Critical Acclaim for
Elizabeth A. Havey's
A Mother's Time Capsule

A thought-provoking and tender collection. In "Thaw," Havey conveys the discomfort of emotional trauma that can inhabit intimate space. We see the different paths individuals take to process grief and are reminded that the best thing we can do is be available for each other. —Mary B. Eigel, author of *Silent Courage: My Lifelong Journey Through Pain to Wellness*

"While reading this collection, I felt like I was in Havey's time capsule, living her characters' stories. Her words brought back treasured memories as if she were talking to me on the phone." — Gay Lynn Essig, teacher and mother of three

Enjoy!

Elizabeth A. Havey

A MOTHER'S TIME CAPSULE

SHORT STORIES ABOUT MOTHERHOOD

BY

ELIZABETH A. HAVEY

For my husband, John,
and for the children of my dreams and my life,
Caroline, Christine and Andrew.

ACKNOWLEDGMENTS

Thanks to John for his constant belief and encouragement. To Jeannine Bergers Everett for reading and commenting—the stories came to life with her help. And to Susan Taylor Chehak, who has generously shared her insight and ideas during the University of Iowa Summer Writing Workshops and beyond. Such mentoring kept me writing and helped me learn my craft. So here I am.

"But behind all your stories is your mother's story, for hers is where yours begins." —Mitch Albom, *For One More Day*

So thanks, Mom, wish you were here to see this.

Someday It Will Be December

In the depths of July, Claire Emmerling began to think about sex. Constantly. In the dense smoke of blue moonlight trailing along her bed, the child within her waxing stronger with kicks so definable she wanted to cry out "hey;" on the maternity unit where with gloved fingers she worked labeling tubes of maroon blood; and always in the garden, the knees of her pants thick with dirt, her ungloved hands busy cultivating, raking away leaves and slack weeds—pulling, tugging. Then she would sit back on her heels and think about his hands upon her.

Did this obsession start with her prenatal classes? Claire signed up and started Lamaze early, a positive sign that *yes* the pregnancy was real. Because at first she had been in complete denial, not believing that any of this was truly happening, feelings of ambiguity preventing her from seeing an OB until she was 20 weeks.

But the denial stage was over, she now in thrall to the pregnancy, to the words her Lamaze instructor spoke: *hormones, secretions, dilatation, cervix, vagina.* Were these very words the cause? Or possibly *massage, comfort, heartbeat*—words throbbing in her head hour after hour.

During the class, she rubbed her belly, and Ana, who sometimes came along as a *partner* rubbed it too.

Effleurage the instructor called it, sheer concentration, sheer attention to Claire's body. Absolute focus on the growth of the baby taking over her heart, her mind, the cells of her skin, the pattern of her breathing, all of it arcing back to why it all was—that time with him.

These thoughts made her turn in to herself, her womanly smells, the scent of her mucus like earth, like the soil of her gardening. No more periods with the odor of blood. In some way it was a virginal state—she set apart, but now because of the child, not because no one desired her. For someone actually had.

During one Lamaze class, she wanted to turn to the women, look at them intently, and exchange these personal feelings about her body, hoping to create a strong bond with each of them. But when she turned to speak to the woman beside her, she saw maternity pants of flowing turquoise silk, not flood-length jeans; she saw gold bracelets, a thick diamond on tanned fingers, a tan so perfect it was probably generated by a machine.

Would this woman want to talk about odors, understand Claire's desire to share? Could they form a bond? She felt a rush of hesitation. Yet she knew they had and would have so much in common: Montgomery's tubercles on their nipples, stretch marks, hemorrhoids, backaches, bladder infections. And sleepless nights.

So she did say something—suggesting they exchange phone numbers, that maybe they could practice breathing together. More words flowed—Claire telling the women she was an L&D nurse at the Chicago Tertiary Care Center, *well not a nurse exactly,* she worked on the unit and for almost a year now, so she knew a lot about labor and delivery. Perhaps they could sit and chat. And from the conversations that followed she got the phone numbers of three different class members.

That night as she lay awake wishing for sleep, she tried not to think of him, of Dr. Christian Farr, of the very night they made this baby. It was safer to remember Steven Arch, a young doctor whom Christian had mentored, remember when he sat at her desk and boldly said that Claire and Christian should be together. "I know this about you both. I'm intuitive, a gift I possess. You and Christian are already one on many levels, so intimacy should be yours."

But Claire had stayed silent. Yes, she wanted to tell Steven that his words made her joyful, but she was hesitant and careful with anything related to Dr. Farr. She only smiled and grasped Steven's hands—a way to relay a belief in his words. And from then on their friendship deepened. For certain, he knew all, while no one else even guessed.

But there was no intimacy with Christian. For here was Claire, in a farmhouse 60 minutes from the hospital, living alone, except for those times when Christian's daughter, Ana, fled his Lake Forest house to be away from her father. With Claire she was free to play her guitar and sing her songs and be angry. Normal for some sixteen-year-olds.

Claire yawned and stretched, beginning her nightly fantasy, conjuring a nameless man whose body might mingle with hers, whose fingers might touch ever so gently, a fantasy necessary for her newly found sex obsession. But this night it finally happened—flashes of her lovemaking with Christian, memories of that single night, rose to the surface. And she did not stop them. Lying in a half sleep, she could almost feel his body humming with warmth against her, his kisses deep and warm, until she reached out and felt the flat coolness of the sheet, instantly becoming awake and aware. Yes: that one night. That night against the length of years when there had been no one beside her, only she in the sheets, single and silent.

Gentle tears came. Her child turned and moved. But the memories of that March night kept on—Christian's fingers, amazingly soft, stroking, touching her everywhere and the spell of that spring night dazzling the sheen of her arms, her back, awakening her body and her life with the damp breeze and a man's caress; and his lying beside her in a tangle, the glow of night just beyond the bed, the careless levels of the thrown-open windows in the bedroom, the movement of white curtains twisting and snapping their lengths. And Claire, finally able to rest her eyes on Christian Farr's legs entwined in hers—and wonder, simply wonder.

And finally Claire slept. But those stunning memories came alive again in her dreaming, so that on awakening, the desire to open the flood-gates of those lovemaking moments and share them with Christian made her reach for the phone. But of course she didn't call him. Yes, their shared conversations and quick cups of coffee between surgeries held weight for her, but to her detriment, she had always hid her feelings. But certainly, he knew what those feelings were.

She sat on the edge of her bed staring at the phone and realizing that yes, though she was not with him, he was there—just beyond, within her reach. She felt that way. And when she changed it around, that he wouldn't be there, she could hardly move, her breath frozen. *Christian, we have this child together. We are in so many ways devoted to each other. We should be together.*

That fecund July stirred other memories for Claire—the faces and bodies of two young people who stopped by her farmhouse almost three years ago. They needed to use her telephone because of car trouble, and they were enthralled, in love.

Standing in Claire's doorway, their bodies touched side to side, hands joined, like two willows bending toward the same stream. Claire invited them in and after making the call, the man took his love's hand in the soft light of the kitchen, held her gaze for long moments—time important only to them and no once else existing. Claire, caught up in their moment, found she was holding her breath.

Pure enchantment was what the two had, and the encounter wedged an image in Claire's mind that she could not shake, that often came to her when hearing the word *love*. And she and Christian?

Claire hungered for what the young lovers had, but bore the pain of knowing that though she and Christian had made a baby that March night, he was set apart from her. She was almost forty, he leaning into his sixties. He would never be hers. He would never come to her bed again. His attentions were clearly defined, a neurosurgeon totally immersed and devoted to his work, connected to her only through that work. Yes she had been his assistant and secretary for fifteen years. But the pregnancy made her flee from him to work in Labor and Delivery. And if his daughter Ana came and stayed at Claire's farmhouse for months at a time—what should have brought the two adults closer together, only drove them farther apart.

Claire had a history of practicing denial, so before, it came naturally that she pretend nothing was happening in her body—this her only shield, her only protection.

Then on a Saturday night in late June, alone in her farmhouse, Claire suddenly thought of the photograph, the Polaroid—as if it had wafted from a tree in her woods, floated through a window into her quiet kitchen.

The Polaroid first surfaced after her parents drowned. She had to clean out their things, sell their house. The very act of walking into their bedroom felt like invasion despite the fact that they were gone, had been buried for months, the bedroom door shut against memories.

All Claire did initially was strip the bed, balling up the sheets that still smelled of cigarette smoke and the musk of her parents' bodies. Balling up the sheets and slamming the bedroom door on the dressing table and bottles of perfume, on the room-length closets, doors ajar, silky gowns dripping from hangers, one tumbling in a mist of lavender on the floor. She could almost hear the moans and groans of her mother, feel again her own body shaking as her young self huddled alone on the top stair—wanting her parents, needing her parents in the dark, in the night, while her mother rose to orgasm in the silent house.

The washing machine had chugged and hummed, Claire's back up against the cold white metal, her shoulders shuddering with sobs in unison to vibrations of the machine that seized the flakes of skin cells, the stains of lovemaking, the last and faintest traces of her parents and washed them away. The dark but fruitful night—holding the promise of spring, luring, pulling at life under a loud boastful moon, *and* the black water, had taken them both.

The final report was still not final—"No one was

there. All of this is conjecture," the police detective told her.

For some reason, her parents went up to the cottage for the weekend and the moon shone and they took out the boat. Claire knew that her mother must have stood in the boat, done something silly, maybe ripping off her clothing—and fell in. The water would squeeze the heart—cold, frigid grip. Her father would go right in after her, plunging down into the water, thinking it would be easy to save her, then thinking he might not be able to save her, then knowing that he would die trying to save her because he couldn't live any other way. But there were times when Claire turned it on its head—her father stood up in the boat to cry out some historical or poetic speech to the moon and tumbled in, maybe hitting his head on the side of the boat when he went down. Her mother threw herself after, not thinking to save him, but to cling to his body, wrap her shaking, icy self around him so that they would be taken together.

The Polaroid was in her father's top dresser drawer, not buried, but floating on top of a pile of neatly pressed handkerchiefs: her mother, naked, pregnant, standing with her back against the closet door, her hands down at her sides, her body angled to emphasize the roundness of her belly, the swelling of her breasts; her mother smiling at her father taking the picture. Of course she was pregnant with Claire. But the picture was of a sexual being, not her mother; Claire had gripped it, her face on fire, trying to take in the revelation. She had never seen her living mother naked. And this was a picture of a woman now dead.

So on that June Saturday night Claire remembered (while lying awake, just beginning to feel infinitesimal movements in her belly) and true understanding opened in her. The baby of the Polaroid, Claire, was incidental to the sex—and the child that moved within her was everything—the sex incidental. Of course, of course.

And Claire would grab on to her child and move forward, move in a direction entirely different from her mother's—her focus her child. She would be a true mother.

So she had heaved herself out of bed and fumbled in the dark for the phone book. This was the end of denial. Yes, she had been trying to hide her pregnancy from everyone in L&D, but now hers and Christian's child could not, would not be denied. She left a message on Dr. Spectra's machine, Spectra being one of the OBs at the Chicago Tertiary Care Center.

An ultrasound was done, pronouncing the baby healthy, giving Claire a due date of December 5th and a list of everything Claire knew Spectra would advise— prenatal vitamins, the name of a childbirth instructor and the suggestion that Claire select a labor partner and learn Lamaze.

"I'm a little concerned about your advanced age, first pregnancy. I would like to do some tests to make sure the baby is developing properly. And I want you to avoid stress, eat well, get a lot of rest and report any unusual occurrences to me immediately."

Though Claire had told none of her fellow workers, the nurses on the unit crowded around her the next day.

"Got any news for us? Anything new in your life?"

They were smiling and warm, offering Claire a hot cup of tea and pulling the desk chairs close to her computer. It was clear that they were not going anywhere until Claire spilled her news.

"I don't have any news," Claire said, the baby suddenly moving as if to encourage her to share, to feel excitement and discard her fears.

"This is a huge hospital, but there are wheels within wheels and fires within fires," the charge nurse said.

Claire blushed. Did they know about Christian? Had that information leaked out? The baby kicked. She held fast. "Yes, hospital equals gossip."

"Claire, Shelley works on our unit, but she also works for Dr. Spectra and saw your name on the appointment list as a prenatal. We know you're pregnant! Congratulations."

Though tears clouded her eyes, Claire saw her future unveiled. It flashed brightly before her, mother and child locked in *love,* two willows bending. And she rose suddenly, embracing each of the nurses, a shroud of worry slipping from her shoulders.

"I'm happy," she mumbled against Shelley's chest. "I'm scared, but I'm going to have this baby and I'm happy."

"Who's the lucky father?" Diane asked quietly.

Claire willed herself to stay calm. What would they all think if they knew it was Christian Farr? But they didn't know. They couldn't know.

"I'm a single mom, Diane, and I plan to keep it that way."

"Got it. But if you need help, there are a lot of us here with lots of experience."

"This a change of life baby?" someone else teased.

"Well it's certainly going to change my life," Claire replied. Laughter. Then everyone gradually split off, walking back to the rooms of their assigned patients, leaving a sense of completeness and yet some emptiness in Claire, who turned back to her computer to enter lab values, do her work.

At the end of summer, as Claire's belly ripened like the fruit on the trees near her farmhouse, her desire for sex waned, her desire to meet her child increasing. On days off, she would walk down her road and on into Prophetstown, enjoying the movements of her child and the soft breezes that played in her hair.

Sometimes she would meet a woman from Lamaze and they would stop and chat, exchange symptoms or discuss due dates. When Claire complained to one that none of her clothes fit, the classmate suggested she use a seamstress in town. This woman could let out some of Claire's skirts and pants. "Continue down this street to Elm and go left. She's in the building next to the barbershop—3221. Here—" and the classmate scribbled the address on a store receipt.

As she turned onto Elm, searching for the address, Claire looked up to see the sun illuminating the figures of four people—a mother, father and a two toddlers snug in a double stroller. The family was just steps ahead and not in any hurry, so Claire moved around them, nodding and smiling as she passed.

But when she came to the address she'd been given, there was no barbershop, no seamstress. So she turned back, only to encounter the family again, ahead of her on the other side of Elm.

Suddenly she wondered if she'd lost her sense of direction. And her thoughts ran on: this family knew theirs—an ordained route, a strolling stance; the mother's head angled to search the sky, her perfect skin shining, a tight mass of curly brown hair tied back against the wind and her feet taking her briskly forward. Claire stopped to stare. Could she simply hail this woman, this mother, and get directions: "Where do I go to be like you?" "What do I do to find a life where even taking a walk fulfills a purpose, has meaning?"

Then the husband stopped and suddenly lifted one of the toddlers out of the stroller, spinning her pink jacket against the startling blue of the late summer sky. Tears bit at the corners of Claire's eyes. But she raised her head and walked on. She would reorient herself. She would find her way.

Facts of Life

Cara informs me that I love the "stupid chair cushion" more than I love her. I immediately apologize for making her cry as I sponge the thick raspberry jam from the light gold fabric.

She just isn't careful anymore, as if the imperfections in our situation now allow for carelessness. Allen's leaving ripped a hole in our life, but I can't allow that to linger and destroy what is left. The car needs a major tune-up. The bottom of the refrigerator leaks. Even our bodies reveal the strain—Cara has had a series of colds and flu and asks for nothing more than to stay on the couch and watch television, her haven from the world. Then, hoping we won't have another argument:

"Sweetie, you have to get dressed. You've got twenty minutes before the bus."

"But I don't feel good." She's not whining, this a clear statement. But she doesn't turn to look at me, instead comforting herself by twisting a strand of hair around a finger and focusing on the panting dog in the cartoon.

"Cara, you're going today. The doctor says you're fine now."

"I think I should stay home another day."

"You have to hand in your bat report, remember?

Those creatures are in my dreams now."

"I can't. I'm still getting over—" She turns to look at me, her brown eyes filling with tears. I get the message, but it's been almost a year now.

"You cover a lot of material in 4th grade, Cara. You don't want to fall behind." I lean over and kiss her damp eyelids. "Why don't you wear your new blouse?"

"You just want to go to work." She says this as I steer her toward her bedroom.

"Yes, I do. Don't you understand that it's absolutely necessary that I work?"

"I don't like any of this," and she flops onto her bed, rolling back into the covers.

I keep going, take her blouse out of the closet only to find it's wrinkled and there's a spot on the collar.

"Cara, up now, please. Fix your hair and get everything else on. I'll iron this."

She rolls toward the bedside table to grab her brush, instead succeeding in knocking over an empty water glass. I hurry out, finding the living room silent— the cartoon characters having just pushed a simple plot to its inevitable conclusion. For a second I want to sink down on the couch too, laugh at a panting dog or anything that fills the screen. But I snap it off and drag the ironing board out of the closet, spinning it into position. "Things are going to be just fine, damn it," I say aloud.

Once at work, my small but tidy office offers sanctuary. Closing my door, I expel the ritual sigh, thankful for this 8:30-5:00 job, for a commuter train that is only a block from my apartment and for co-workers who leave me alone. All this allows me to work without interruption, make my calls, attend to endless mail so my day won't be extended and make me late getting back to Cara.

But today is different. When at ten o'clock I go to the cafeteria to glance at the newspaper and consume a mug of coffee and a roll, the place is unusually crowded. My colleagues are all gathered at one table discussing a party that our supervisor has decided to throw.

"He's really pleased with how we turned our numbers around last month," Chuck says to me. "He's even giving this thing at his house. So unlike him."

I smile and find a place at the end of their table. I want to be friendly, but my decisions are always about time. I keep quiet, sip coffee, my thoughts immediately traveling to Cara. I picture how she looked when the bus finally arrived. I go through my litany: yes, she has her house key, lunch, books. But regardless, a hollow feeling of dread grows at the back of my mind. I keep waiting for it to reach full-bloom so I'll finally know what it is I've forgotten to do for her, what exactly she is missing.

"Anne, can you make it on Saturday?" Mark asks this from across the table. I knew he was there, choosing a seat directly across from me. I also assume, without looking, that he is eating a carton of plain yogurt. Whenever I see him in the cafeteria, that's what he's eating. I look up from my jelly doughnut, wishing I didn't have sugar sticking to my fingers.

"It sounds like fun." I say this, then realize how dull I sound. Conversation seems to stick in my throat in these man-and-woman exchanges. I am so out of practice. Brushing my sugary fingers on a paper napkin, I give him my best smile. "Yes, I'm going." The words are out before I have really thought them through. Then another reflex kicks in—I rise and gather my things.

"I'll pick you up then, if that's okay. Around eight?"

I feel trapped. We've had coffee together two or three times. We've waited for the train together. He asked me out once, but Cara got sick and I cancelled.

My reflex smile: "Thanks, Mark, really, but I've got to pick up a sitter and I think it would be better if I drove myself. "

I escape, hurrying to the elevator. My desk is waiting with so much to sort out. And then there's my life. My life. No man is going to rescue me, or make me race around on a Saturday to be ready by eight o'clock. And maybe I'll skip it—Cara and I could take the train downtown to the zoo, later cuddle on the couch with pizza and a movie.

Cara isn't on her bike at the station when I get off the train. The September sky is still bright and I walk the short block home searching for some reason for her absence. Maybe she stopped to play ball in the thick fall grass. Maybe she is sitting on the porch of our four-flat with Mrs. Riley. But when I reach the apartment there are no children around. I find her in front of the television.

"Is the table set, Young Lady, have you done all your homework?" I'm ready for a fight. Why can't she hold up her end of the deal? She doesn't look sick. Slowly she untangles herself from the couch cushions and stands, holding me and burying her face in my jacket.

"Cara," I say, that hollow dread growing again, "is something wrong?"

"I don't know anything. A lot of things."

"Give me one thing."

"I don't know what a sexpot is."

I want to giggle with relief, but I don't. She's been asking some of the right questions lately, but I'm simply not ready to set out all the facts. I really don't want to talk about any of it—especially the past and Allen. We move apart and I start toward the kitchen saying, "Sexpot. Now who in your class is going around talking about that?"

"Tom Brody. He said I was a sexpot. But I'm not fat, Mom, and I don't look anything like a pot. I don't get it."

"Tom Brody was saying something he heard his father say. He probably doesn't know what it means either. Being called a sexpot doesn't mean you're fat. It means you're pretty, but not in a way I like to hear. Tom Brody probably likes you—"

"Mom," Cara says with complaint in her voice, "I don't think you know what it means either. And do we have to have spaghetti again?"

But I just turn to the boxes and jar on the counter, feeling relieved and suddenly very hungry.

During dinner Cara and I discuss what we should buy for Lucy Baxter who is having a birthday party in two weeks.

"I've been invited to a party too," I say. "It's this Saturday night. People from work."

She looks up, her hair falling in her face. I must cut her bangs. I must get the spot out of her blouse because it has to last this season.

"Mom. Please don't go, okay, please?"

On the train tonight, I had more time to think things through. I should go to this party. It's better for me to get out and not always be focusing on my child. I concentrate on buttering a roll, saying in my firmest voice, "Cara, I'd really like to go. We'll be together all day Sunday. I promise."

"Don't you feel funny going to a party without Dad?"

I look up at her and our eyes lock. She hasn't mentioned Allen since his last breezy phone call when Cara asked him where he was. He evaded and talked about the Christmas present she would be getting. When the call was over, I tried to blot out the promise, saying that her Dad was too carefree, not very organized, that he had a hard time holding his life together. I never want her to count on him. But in this situation, he's her only weapon.

"Your dad and I—he's been gone a long time now."

"I know." She is blinking tears. "I don't love him anymore anyway, except when I remember his hugs, then I do."

Quickly I push away from the table, that hollow dread fully-grown and consuming me.

"Cara, I love you so." It is all I can manage as we stare at each other. Then I pick up my plate and move to the kitchen. She finishes her dinner and we don't speak of the party again. After her shower, we play beauty shop. I cut her bangs and work silky lotion into her back and arms. We go over the spelling words that are giving her trouble. Ecstasy - e-c-s-t-a-s-y. "Remember there are two s's and no x," I tell her.

"What does it mean?" she asks, suddenly hugging me around the waist and burying her head in my lap.

"It means that everything is wonderful—that you're just about as happy as you can be," I say, thinking what a gift in my life she truly is. Then Cara is laughing, "Look at the mess you've made, Mom.

There's hair all over the rug, and you just knocked over the lotion."

Hours later, after I have kept myself busy with laundry and lunches, there is nothing left to do. I wander the apartment turning lights on and then turning them off. The comforting dark that once surrounded Allen and me as we clung to each other has become a maze of shadows that I'm trying to find my way through.

Once in bed, with the covers tightly around me, I feel safe. A song is playing softly on the radio, an old song and the words come back easily. But in some way they are different and I can't decide why. But the more I puzzle over it, the reason is clear—the lyrics are boldly talking about sex, about coupling, intercourse, fucking, and yet when I was young, like Cara, I didn't get it. I didn't hear that underlying urge, the rougher edges. The song only communicated excitement and closeness, part of falling in love. Once Allen and I had that, but in the end he was no protection from the darkness—I held us both up.

I turn off the radio, thinking how jaded I've become. Cara's question about sexpot comes back to me; half asleep, the fatigue of the day taking over, I pretend I am her age, wrestling with the word myself, struggling to visualize it. All that forms in my mind is something round and soft. Sexpot. Maybe my own mother, her belly, when as a kid I needed comfort and plunged my head into her warm, apron-covered lap. Yes, that's it. I fall asleep.

The next day there is a note on my desk. "*Anne, let*

me pick you up on Saturday. I'll stop for your sitter first. Please think about it, Mark."

I set the note aside. I have to deal with Cara's insecurity and neediness; I have to talk to her again about this party.

During the day I don't see him. I avoid the cafeteria and instead walk a fast mile during my lunch break. At the end of the day I hurry and catch an earlier train, hoping that Cara will be there to meet me. She is, but my heart lurches when I see the frightened expression in her eyes. Hiding my concern, I hug her. "How was your day, Sweetie?"

"Mom," she says standing still, not moving to get on her bike. "We had a very scary day. A kidnapper."

The air crackles with her words. My hands on her shoulders dig in as if to reassure myself that she is there. "Come on, Sweetie, let's walk and you can tell me all about it." Her words come fast, rushing and confused as the talk of an excited child often is.

"One of the younger kids, I don't know what grade. Linda Leonardo. Mrs. Dorsey's room. She's young and stupid and didn't know about strangers. Well that's what I think and that's what Mrs. Leeman said, the part about strangers. Cause there was this man and he had a car parked near school. But not near where we get off the bus. He had his car and she came along and he tried to show her something. He tried to grab her arm, pull her into his car. But she screamed and got away and ran toward the playground. So I guess she was brave, right? And not stupid. To scream, I mean. I don't know if I would be that brave. And they got the police going all over the neighborhood and they caught the stranger."

"They caught him. You're sure," I say realizing Cara was at the train by herself.

"Yes. We had to stay after school. The bus was late. On purpose. And all the teachers were giving us these talks. And reminding us about strangers and stuff. Mrs. Leeman said things I didn't really understand, but—"

I wonder why someone didn't call me. Or maybe Cara has a note in her backpack. Panic is washing over me. We are almost home and I'm shaking; it's over and we're going inside to have a quiet evening and I'm shaking.

"I think I'm okay, Mom. Really."

I get the door unlocked. Cara goes around the back to put her bike away and I race through the hall into the kitchen so that I can watch her out the window.

When she comes in, she asks: "Mom, do men always want to hurt people?"

"No, Cara, no, no. There are wonderful men in the world. There are men who love their children and want to take care of them and their wives. They go to work every day to take care of their families. Like Lucy's dad. That man today was sick, sick in his head. There are people like that. And there are people like, like—"

"Like my Dad."

"Yes, Cara. Your father loves you; but love also means caring about the day-to-day things, being responsible for those you love. He's not good at the responsibility part." She is holding on to every word. "Please believe me, men are good and loving someone is good and getting married and having babies is good."

I kiss her, wind my fingers gently in her hair. She is such a visual reminder of my connection to Allen.

"One thing Mrs. Leeman kept telling us. It wasn't Linda Leonardo's fault. It wasn't her fault about the man. But I knew that right away. And it wasn't my fault about Dad."

My fingers fall from her hair. "It wasn't your fault. Ever."

We don't talk about it anymore and she doesn't ask any questions about the things she doesn't understand. I'm glad. I just want to change the subject.

When Cara is finally asleep, I go into the bathroom to get ready for bed. In my nakedness, I shiver, not for lack of heat. How sexless it was in my childhood when my brother and I would bathe in the same tub—he in the front, me in the back, water sloshing around us, water down our backs and fronts in a water fight—until, until I was budding and he was not. Until I was beginning and he was not. Sexpot. Sex. No more baths together, my mother said. Innocence swirling down the drain with the water. Much later Allen and me in the tub—but I don't want to be rescued by memories of his attentions—by anyone's attentions.

When I fall into bed, there's the water of tears on my face. I cry for Cara, for myself. I cry for my loneliness and for Linda Leonardo and the fear she must have felt and I even cry for the man who is so horribly wrong. Life can get so out of control and here I am trying to keep some order in our lives. Cara deserves the fleeting innocence.

Then I stop myself. Aren't we really doing fine? But the answer is filled with negative memories: Allen's angry yelling fits, Cara's nightmares, my own blind fears. Silence becomes so tactile in my room that I can hear it. Wide-awake, I lie listening for a long time, then try to block out the silence by making a resolve—I will talk to Cara about sex and love. I have to. There are so many connections.

Then a memory of when she was four, rises. Every

night she said three prayers, baby prayers that we taught her. Once at the end of this routine, she said flatly: "All people are special and we should let them into our house. Amen." I quickly tucked her in and went to tell Allen, wondering about the source of such a statement. Being more interested in the baseball game he was watching, Allen merely shrugged, blind to innocence once again.

If Cara's belief in people was shaken today, I know it's still there, despite this scary episode. I'm the one that's no longer convinced. I roll over reaching for sleep.

In the morning, Cara doesn't suggest any changes in her routine, so I watch her get on the bus and gratefully go to work. On one of my breaks I go to the cafeteria. Mark is there. I get a coffee, a tidy croissant and sit across from him.

"I think it's a good day. It's Friday."

"Are you okay, Anne, you look like some pale breeze."

"I'm okay." I breathe the answer and then find it hard to know where to settle my eyes. I want to look at him, want to find some comfort in his grin or the wrinkles around his eyes that appear when he's totally involved in what he's saying. Instead, I stare down at his yogurt.

"Cara had a problem at school yesterday." I stop.

"What happened?" He reaches over and touches my hand.

"She's all right. Really. But that's why I'm pale. Didn't sleep well. I should have eaten breakfast—"

"I'll go over and get you some eggs."

"No. Mark." The words are almost angry. I try

again. "No. Thank you. But no. I'm fine." I try to soften things by smiling. I pull my hand gently away. "I'm behind schedule, so I think I'll get back to it."

I find myself standing. Decision made. I wave and hurry out, back to my office. We didn't speak of the party tomorrow. I'll deal with it later. I have work to do.

Saturday I wake early. I like Saturdays, especially in spring and fall when birdsong comes through my open window and lovely streams of sunlight touch my quilt.

I walk to the window. The sky is azure blue. There are red leaves on the grass. Autumn is brilliant and it thrills me, makes me eager. Cara and I might go to the park. We might—and then unexpectedly a dull ache fills me. It's Saturday and it will be Saturday night.

Before I can talk myself out of it, I head to the living room, reach for the phone as I search in my directory for Mark's number.

"Who are you calling?" Cara asks. She's been watching cartoons and when I look over at her, she looks as impish as a blue Smurf.

"I'm calling Mark from work. I'm going to ask him to pick me up for the party tonight." I think I'm saying this with firm certainty.

"I don't want you to go. I told you. Why do you want to go with him anyway? You don't really know him. I mean I don't know him."

I turn and look at her. "That's true. You've never met him. But I know he's kind and looks out for me at work. And—"

I stop, wanting to examine and weigh what I know and don't know about Mark—that he was married once before, but it didn't work out and there were no children. That he has a great smile, that when he's around I want to say the right thing, feel comfortable because I'm a woman and he's a man. I also realize that what I do know makes me long to pick up the phone, learn more about him.

Cara gets off the couch, walks over to me. "Are you going to call him, are you?" Her voice is all nervous and edgy. I also hear a challenge in it.

"Yes, I am. And maybe—"

I stop. What was I going to say, some stupid promise about the future, something that would include Cara?

"Do you love him, Mom?" She's looking up at me, again twisting strands of her hair around her fingers.

"No. Cara. He's a friend. I'm only going to a party with him. People from work. It's just—"

"Mom." Her voice shakes. "Some kids at school keep asking me if you have a boyfriend. Sarah, I don't like her, she's in the 7th grade and argued with me, said that you had a boyfriend and that her mother does. That one morning when she went to cuddle with her mom he was there in her mom's bed. She said it's the facts of life. She said it would happen to me."

My God, why do people have to interfere in our lives? Can't they just leave us alone?

I move to the kitchen counter, reach to hold the edges with my hands, anger rolling over me. Then I feel her standing next to me and I know with a certainty that I have never felt before that what I say to her now is crucial. I turn and hug her, thinking over and over, no more hurts, no more.

"Why didn't you tell me about this before? Why didn't you let me know that you were afraid something like that would happen?"

"I don't know."

"Talk to me."

"I was tired. I was tired of thinking about it. I didn't want to talk about it. I just didn't want to!"

I am amazed at how her feelings echo mine. The two of us avoiding again and again.

"What happened to Sarah, what she told you—don't worry. I'm your mother. I love you first. And if I ever love another man, you'll love him too. We'll find all of this together. I'll tell you things. Don't be afraid. Trust me, please."

"But I want things to stay as they are." She is frantic. She clutches my arm and I know what I have done in the last year is good. I'm building something for her that she doesn't want to lose.

"Things are going to be all right, I promise. Things are good with us, just the two of us. We are happy now. I love being with you. And I am so proud of how you are growing. You teach me about lots of things like bats and butterflies, funny jokes and skateboard moves. And if you are tired of spaghetti, I'll teach you how to cook. We can make decisions together. But Cara, if you get to go to Lucy's party, then I get to go out too. You get to grow up. I get to do what adults do. That's the deal."

She nods and hugs me fiercely as I look toward the phone.

It is an Indian summer evening with a full moon forming and the sun going down in orange streaks. Cara and I can't decide what we want for supper, so instead we take a long walk immersing ourselves in the falling leaves and descending twilight. When I called Mark that morning, he didn't answer. I did leave a message on his answering machine. I cancelled the sitter. Cara's spirits have been unusually high ever since.

When we round the corner to our apartment, we

see someone sitting on the building steps. Mark rises and comes out of the shadows. As I introduce him to Cara, he smiles and holds out two white bags, their tops neatly folded.

"I took a chance you'd be here. Have you two ladies eaten?"

Immediately I look to Cara, wondering how this will go. But still caught up in the flow of this splendid evening, she surprises me and reaches for one of the white bags, giggling.

"Don't get too excited, Cara, it's probably plain yogurt," I say light-heartedly and then hang back, wanting to know if Mark got my phone message.

We each open a bag revealing French fries and cheeseburgers.

"That's exactly what I wanted," Cara says matter-of-factly and I decide it is what I want too.

We sit at the picnic table in the backyard and I bring out glasses, lemonade and a chilled bottle of sparkling water. As we eat, Cara takes over most of the conversation. In detail she tells Mark about her school and the skateboard moves she wants to learn, until a few of her friends from up the street wander into the yard. After a quick exchange of what's been happening in the neighborhood, they run off to play in the lingering light. Mark extends his hand across the table and I reach for it.

"Last time we talked, I mentioned a problem Cara had at school."

"Yes—"

"I'm not used to sharing."

"It's okay, I get it. She's lovely, by the way. Strong. Resilient, like her mother."

"Not always. A stranger near her school tried to lure a child into his car."

"That's the worst. No wonder you— But everything is okay, the child is okay?"

"Yes. And they caught the guy."

"A bad day for both of you."

"Yes. And then there was an older girl—" I hesitate. I'm just not used to looking into this man's eyes, but I plunge on, "An older girl warning Cara that some day she'll go to crawl into bed with me and there will be a man there."

We are silent, hands lingering. Mark says: "I would tell her that such an event won't happen until both of you want it to. I would guess you might need Cara's consent if some man wanted to be your husband and her father."

"Yes."

"Anne, tonight—I won't stay for very long."

"Could we just go slowly?" He nods. We are reading each other's minds. We talk some more and then he rises, saying, "If it's okay with you, I'll go down the street and find Cara. It's almost dark."

Up in the apartment I stand at the window for a moment. I stare down at the lawns, seeing the children playing in the fading light, hearing tangles of words and shouts coming from the darkening shrubbery. And I find I am clutching my fingers into my palm, I am holding on to something. It is the day, the evening I am cherishing—these moments right now. And I am falling back in time, seeing myself down on the lawn playing, my brother too, we ignoring the calls of mother and father to come home, instead moving and weaving in and out of the trees, playing hide and seek and shouting and laughing endlessly. Fireflies light up the memory and we are reaching for them with fingers and running

27

as their lights streak the night. Then mother calls us back into the brightness of our house and I hear the gushing of running tub water—the almost perfect beginnings of my life.

I hear Mark and Cara talking and laughing as they come up the stairs. I turn on lights, the shadows fall away and I stand smiling at them.

"Cara knows everything there is to know about fireflies and mosquitoes and bats," Mark says. "She has all the facts."

Cara runs and hugs me and I hold her, knowing that now I will always tell her things she needs to know about life—her life and mine.

Fragile

"I'm going to take you to Devil's Lake after this business trip," Adam says, sorting through some papers on his desk.

"Sounds ominous," Tess laughs. She has helped him pack his suitcase and now stands in a streak of July sunshine. It is 6:00 a.m.

"Rich told me about it. Perfect spot for the camper." He finishes assembling papers and shuts his briefcase. Tess walks into his arms.

"The lake is surrounded by towering ridges of granite. Rich says it's almost mountainous." He kisses her and gives her his favorite bear hug.

"Stop, Adam," Tess giggles, "you'll crack a rib."

They drop arms and smile at each other. "Tell my girls about the camping trip." He plants a firm kiss on her forehead.

"I will. Be safe."

"Hey, I just get on the plane. I don't even think about it. See you in four days."

She smiles, waving him out of the room. She won't follow him to the door or watch as the car pulls away. She will stay still, warmed by the sunlight, until she hears a final honk as he goes up the road.

Moments later there are footfalls above and she

hurries toward the stairs. Sara is coming down, rubbing her eyes. Tess meets her halfway and eagerly takes her into the kitchen. While she pours juice for the child, she tells her how early it is and that Sara should go back to bed. This is another ritual. Both of them know there is no going back. Sara has been like this since birth; movements in the house awaken her and she pops her head up, struggling out of sleep. From the bedroom doorway, Tess has watched the four-year-old almost stumble as she slips from the bed pushing herself into wakefulness.

"You're like Daddy," Tess says patting Sara's gold head. "Impulsive and compulsive—the two of you."

"Let's wake Karen," Sara is already suggesting.

"She'll be up soon. We have a long day ahead of us and your big sister needs her sleep. I'll find something for you to do."

But it is really Tess who needs to keep busy. She can't help looking at the clock and noting, later during Karen's breakfast, that Adam is now at the airport. When *Sesame Street* is over and the girls are eager to go outside, all Tess can see is Adam boarding the plane. She had flown with him a year ago and as she stepped from the jet bridge into the plane, she stared at the thinness of the fuselage—a casing so fragile. Shaking away the memory, she chides herself for worrying, but is already calculating how long Adam will be in the air as she and the children head to the vegetable garden.

"Let's see what we can pick today," she says, working her happy voice. They plow after her into the thick-leaved zucchini plants. All of them find the dark green fruit nestled here and there in the vines. In minutes they have at least six; two days ago they found eight and Tess saw no new ones coming. She marvels. The tiny gold flowers are so delicate and small when the plant is young, but as the leaves grow the strong dark vegetables explode from thin shoots overnight.

"There's tons," Sara is saying.

"That's because it's Mom's garden," Karen says.

"Well thanks. I don't know why they show such strong life. I don't even water them and look."

Karen shrugs, a faint smile curling. Her eight years have taught her that Tess likes to be praised.

At noon Tess turns on the radio, but at the moment the world is calm—no airplane crashes or any other trauma. She flicks it off, scolding herself once again.

The days pass quickly. Tess and the girls always have a busy agenda. They shop for camping supplies, Tess replacing their old lantern with a safer, battery-operated one. Another day the girls beg to go and swim at the pool and so Tess takes them. She pulls a chair to the edge of the baby pool, the shouts and joyous screams of children filling the air. Other mothers form tight clusters to chat and read, but Tess watches intently, pushing away the daymare of a child sinking down into the clear, bright water.

When they arrive home, the UPS driver delivers a package stamped FRAGILE, HANDLE WITH CARE. Tess takes it into the kitchen. She sets the package on the counter, gets a box cutter and eagerly works at the tape. "Yes it is," she says to the girls lifting a ceramic vase in lilac shades. "I ordered this for my garden flowers."

When she walks away with the cutter and wrapping paper, Sara quickly pulls over a chair and climbs up to grab at the vase.

"I want to see, Mama."

"Sara, no," Tess says spinning back to the counter and quickly lifting the vase above the child's head. "The vase is for me and it's breakable. You could cut yourself."

"I just want to see," Sara says. Tess holds the vase out. Sara reaches and strokes it with one finger, then scrambles down from her chair and runs off.

Another day Tess and the girls bake bread. They make large buttery loaves and laugh as the flour covers their hands and arms and poufs into the sunlight. They wrap two loaves for their camping trip and take one down the road to a neighbor who is going to watch the house while they are gone. Coming back they see Adam's car in the drive and the girls rush into the house shrieking and calling out to him. Tess's hand sneaks up to her throat as she hurries after them. She stops at the door, watching him hug the girls in the kitchen. He turns. They smile at each other.

"You're a day early," she says. "You didn't call."

"Life is full of surprises. I couldn't see one of my clients—it can wait. So let's get going. Let's pack the camper and go."

Adam changes into jeans and hitches his car to the camper that is always parked in the garage. He pulls the vehicle into the driveway and the girls line up with pails and cloths to give everything a good washing. Excitement fills the air as they race around giggling and splashing the camper and themselves.

"We'll be on our way tonight, tonight," Adam singsongs with the girls as he starts to crank up the camper to its tented heights. But then the crank sticks and even with the aid of a wrench he cannot make it move. The wrench clatters to the ground. Tess says nothing.

"I know what it is," Adam growls. "Last fall I checked everything over, remember? The chain that pulls the top up looked like it would hold, but obviously it hasn't." The girls are suddenly quiet. Tess walks away into the house, remembering the ticket Adam had to pay when he forgot his front headlight had burned out.

Adam is fortunate to find the necessary parts in town. The camper is repaired; the trip delayed only a day. When they are finally on their way, Tess leans back in the front seat and basks in the thought of the relaxing, uncluttered hours ahead. The car radio buzzes news and weather, but she doesn't need to listen. Adam is driving and when she closes her eyes tightly she can picture the girls' color pages with slashes of strong red crayon or brilliant purple dots. They amuse themselves well and only ask that lunch be a picnic under a tree somewhere.

"Want to drive?" Adam asks her after a while.

"Not really. I will though," Tess adds with a yawn.

Adam laughs.

"What's so funny?"

He turns and smiles at her and she supposes that he would rather drive anyway. He likes every aspect of camping. She is content.

The first night Adam builds a fire. Tess makes sure the girls stay back as they gather in the dark, watching the sparks float upward and dissolve in the smoke.

Adam is gregarious and huddles with the girls telling them about fish, hiking trails, sunsets and granite.

"Those purple rocks we saw when we were driving in?" Karen asks.

"Yes. They rise above the lake. Sometimes they crack and fall. There are lots of rocks along the shore. I'll show you."

"I like purple," Sara says.

"What is granite really?" Karen asks.

Adam leans back against the camper, wrapping his hands around his head. "It's igneous rock, Karen. That means it was formed when the rock was partially on fire or molten. Granite is extremely hard. They build statues with it."

"Wow," Sara breathes. "I don't want to touch it— hot!"

"It's cool now, Baby. Cool and pretty."

Tess smiles, leaning back in her camp chair to watch the stars and listen to their eager voices.

The next day they wander the trails. Tess tires of the bugs and narrow passages but the girls are in awe of Adam and what he shows them—so she goes along. They eat some lunch at the camper and then walk a quarter mile to the lake to swim and gather rocks.

"Why do they call it Devil's Lake? I don't see any devil," Karen says looking at the calm water.

"Stones," Sara says. She points to huge boulders and chunks of granite that rise in piles along the lakeshore. At various points the granite soars in tall tiers above the water.

After they swim and wrap themselves in towels, Adam calls to the girls and they walk off the smooth sand of the beach into the rocky areas. Tess sits dulled by the hot sun. She thinks about picking up her book, but instead watches them picking their way among the rocks, bending, examining and rising again to move forward. Adam is in trunks, his long legs flickering in the dark rock. Tess is surprised to see his legs so white and she considers how good he will look by the end of the week, tanned and rested.

Then she sees him raise a huge stone over his head. She looks for the girls. They are standing off a ways, Karen holding Sara's hand. Adam's back is to them. He awkwardly drops the stone. Tess rises from the sand and shades her eyes to see. She wants to call to them but they are around the bend in the lake and motor-boats ply the water. Tess wonders what Adam is doing. His pale arms are now holding aloft another heavy stone. The afternoon sun strikes the rocks. And then she sees Sara leap forward; it is her popping movement, her eager, purposeful rush. Karen jumps backward and Adam seems to turn all in one jumble of movement. Tess is scrambling through the sand, trying to hear what she thinks she hears—a scream of panic. She has to look down to find her way among the sharp-edged rocks and when she nears them she can hear screaming. It is Adam. He is standing over Sara shouting, "Why did you move? I told you not to move."

Tess passes by Karen who is dulled to stone. Sara lies on the ground, blood trickling down her face. Tess's hands shake as she moves a towel, wipes the blood trying to see where the source of the injury is.

"I told her not to move," Adam says, his voice more subdued now. Tess looks up at him. He is white, his face pinched as if the chunk of granite had struck him.

"We have to get her to a hospital now," Tess says. "Sara, where does it hurt?"

"My eye," the child says trying to touch her face. Tess restrains her. "Adam, go back and get help."

Their eyes meet. "I was only trying to show them something. I didn't hit her with the rock. I don't know what happened. I told her not to move."

"Adam, can you go back?" She is cradling the child now and looking at him. "Adam can you go back to the ranger station, you know, the one right beyond the beach, and get help?"

Sara is conscious. Tess is greatly relieved. But the sun is hot and the very knowledge that they could be out of it soon is really all she can think about.

"I'll take her, give her to me," Adam says suddenly, reaching out for Sara.

"It's too far off, Adam. We shouldn't move her. They'll send an ambulance—it can stop on the north shore road." Tess nods her head in the direction.

"Okay, okay, I'm going back." His voice is mechanical. He starts to move away from them. "Be careful with her, Tess." He stands one more second looking at them and then turns and strides over the rocks. He is in bare feet and Tess wonders how he manages to move so quickly.

Tess covers Sara with a towel. She tries to get the child to tell her what's wrong but Sara can only moan and say Mama over and over.

"Karen, can you tell me what happened?" Tess works to keep her voice steady and calm.

"Daddy was going to break open one of the rocks. I'm not sure why. He wanted to show us something. He likes showing us things. We were only having fun." She breaks down now, crying hard, her body shaking. She is still standing off a way from Tess.

"Of course you were. It's okay, Sweetie. It's going to be okay."

The words feel good in the hot air. Tess holds onto them as she holds onto the listless body of Sara. For a moment, the words block out images of what just happened.

"Is Sara okay? What's going on?" Karen sobs.

"Help will come, Sweetie. We'll get a doctor for Sara and everything will be fine. I know you can be brave right now."

The phrase is foolish, ordinary, but it seems amazingly right. Such words swim in her mind, words and images—Sara's face now white and puffy, Karen's face streaked with dirt and tears, and Adam's helpless look.

They wait. When the ambulance siren travels toward them, Tess stands and soon she is holding Sara out to a paramedic. Adam is already in the ambulance when Tess and Karen get to the road. She helps Karen scramble into the back of the rig and they shoot off. Adam kneels next to Sara's stretcher and grabs her hand. He talks to her while the paramedic carefully cleanses her eye.

Tess takes a seat at the back of the ambulance and cradles Karen in her lap. For a while they hold their places like mannequins in a store window. Karen changes the pattern by falling asleep. Tess slowly looks to Adam, reaches out her hand and touches his shoulder. When he turns, tears are trembling on his face.

They race along, a siren warning of their advance, Tess feeling Karen's heart rapidly beating under her hand. She thinks *this child, the other child*, so dependent on two people who are sometimes sure and often unsure, as each day comes into being and then gradually fades away.

A team with a stretcher meets them in the ambulance bay. Karen snaps awake, her eyes intent and searching. Tess knows that this look does not show capability, but a fierce wish to help. Tess can't ask for anything more—were she to catch her own reflection this very moment, her eyes would speak the same.

A young woman, a park ranger in training, is there with a car. She took care of everything: gathered their things at the beach, brought them clothes from the camper and most importantly is ready to take Karen to a motel room. Tess longs to hold on, to keep Karen close by her side, but she gently guides the child toward this young woman, watches as they take each other's hands and walk away.

At seven p.m. the doctor drops something into Tess's hand. It is a sliver of plum-colored rock. Tess closes her fingers over it and then opens them seeing the jagged lines of color and feeling the rough edges.

"It's so small, fragile…" She looks up at the doctor.

"What can we do?" Adam asks wretchedly. He has been sitting with his head down, using his hand to rumple his hair or peel a callous from his palm. His face is red, from the position and from their morning on the lake.

"It's not your fault, Adam," Tess says. "It was an accident."

"Your daughter is doing fine, still in recovery, not awake yet," the doctor says. "You could go and get something to eat. Then come back and check on your daughter."

Check on your daughter. Tess thinks *Karen.*

"We're lucky, aren't we," Adam says.

The rock cuts into Tess's clenched hand. "It could have done a lot of—" but she stops.

The doctor reaches and touches her shoulder. "It could have severed the optic nerve. But it didn't. So relax."

Tess and Adam fall into step hurrying toward the elevator. They are both thinking of Karen. Eating is out of the question, so they immediately take a silent cab ride to the motel.

The room is dim, the television flickering without sound, light glowing from the tiled bath. The ranger springs quickly from her half-sleep and Tess automatically reaches out and gentles her back into the chair. Adam moves toward the bed to check on Karen. When he kisses her, she mumbles and rolls far over to the edge of the bed. Tess stands staring at the warm indentation in the bedclothes, the nest that Karen had curled into. In the bluish light it is an empty hole with dark twists of sheets. Tess reminds herself that Sara is just fine; then she walks to the other side of the bed, lifts Karen back and gently covers her.

"Now I must see Sara," she says, turning to Adam, her voice cracking.

"Everything will be fine here," the young woman tells them. "I'll stay for as long as you need."

She hands them the keys to her car. "And one more thing. Karen wanted me to tell you. She said she knows what happened."

"Really," Adam says, his voice lifting.

"Yes. Sara just wanted to see."

"See what?" Tess's voice has an edge.

"What her Dad was doing. Karen says Sara's just like that."

They drive in silence for a while, Adam at the wheel, Tess focusing on the road, trying to avoid the image of Sara's puffy-white face, an image that will be with her for a while. She recognizes it not only from this afternoon, but also from daymares that occurred after the incident on the highway last winter. Then, as they were heading home from a Christmas party with the children asleep in the back seat, the car in front of them lost control, spinning in circles and finally pointing right at them, a deadly compass. Adam steered to the left and avoided the vehicle, but somehow for Tess, it has always been lurking there, about to hit them. She shakes her head back and forth, grips her hands into fists. She has pictured too many accidents. It has to stop. Sara is alive. She can see. Sara will be fine.

"Adam. Please say something." Tess's voice is raspy and thin.

"Sorry. I'm thinking. Are you okay?" He glances over at her.

"Yes, but I can't believe I got through it, I mean I held up."

"You did everything right." He leans forward, searches the dark road.

"But it wasn't me. I was there, but it was all happening around me. Still, I held up." The last words are broken by a sob. She is shaking now, the tears released. She fumbles in her purse for a tissue.

"It's okay, Tess."

She gives in to it and then after a while, the tears are unnecessary. She turns back to Adam.

"Can you talk about it now, tell me what you were doing?"

He turns briefly and she sees anger flicker over his face. "I simply wanted to split a rock. I wanted them to see the inside of a piece of granite. That's all."

Tess's body ripples with a shaking sigh.

"It was stupid, very stupid. But I did tell them to

stay back. I did."

"But you know Sara, she's only four. You know how she is. Adam, didn't you even question whether it was safe to—"

"Tess. Please. Now I know it was stupid. But then— You just can't know everything."

His words are her own thoughts. He also feels that dark and silent helplessness. After a while, she reaches over and touches his shoulder.

"Why did you yell at her?"

The question hangs between them for a long while. Than Tess's voice: "It's okay, you don't have to say. I know. I really do know. There are things we can't control."

They are silent for a long time, hurtling into the dark and then Tess begins to talk.

"Sara worries about things. I know she does. I remember one day she was crying in front of the TV and I hurried in to see. She grabbed my hand and asked me if the bear on *Sesame Street* was really going to eat the fish. I told her no, he wasn't. Then she was okay."

"You should have told her the truth. Animals eat other animals. It's part of knowing there are dangers in the world. We aren't always going to be there."

"I struggle with all of it. Sara didn't want to hear that. She and Karen love everything. How can you damage that?"

"We can protect them for so long and then—"

"Then this."

"Tess, can you stop now. I've said how sorry I am. Let's move forward. We're all okay."

Tess weighs his words, thinking maybe they can. Maybe they might even finish their camping trip, if the doctor says it's okay. They could stay on the beach, create sandcastles, eat strawberries and drink lemonade.

She pictures the girls running and shouting, hair catching the sunlight, blue sky all around them. A smile crosses her face and she feels lighter, freer—like the dark breezes that come at her through the car window.

"I like what Sara did. She is Sara and she just wanted to see. Her way is better. She's unafraid and just wants to grab onto life—just grab on. I envy that."

Adam maneuvers the car into a parking place, shuts off the engine and pulls Tess in. "I love you, Tess."

"Give me a bear hug please. Make it a good one and make it crack."

It is one month after the accident. Sara no longer has to wear an eye patch so Tess takes the children to the pool. Summer is ending and the pool is quiet, not crowded. Karen finds some of her friends in the big pool. Tess sits down on the cement by the baby pool to watch Sara.

The child has a large inner tube that she twirls in the water, throwing her head back and laughing as she goes around and around. Tess feels a rush of contentment and leans back to look up at the solid blue sky. It's a hot day, the cement warm under the palms of her hands. When she looks back to Sara's laughing face, she notices the even lines of the blue pool that separate the water from the hot cement. She feels the sun on her skin and suddenly a breeze lifts her dark hair. She thinks—me, Sara, sunshine, that endless, endless sky.

When she tucks the two of them in bed that night, they are exuberant. As she goes down the stairs to be with Adam, they call over and over the words: "Love ya, see ya in the morning, good night. Love ya, see ya in the morning, good night. Love ya…"

Tess stops. She listens, the words falling on her with their weight of wonder. And welcoming all of it, she holds them, keeps them like a charm her two have hung gently around her neck.

Thaw

Her landlord said maybe she'd imagined it. She doesn't think so. They argued about the age of the townhouse, the condition of the roof. She was late for her shift and had to hang up. "You're the one with squirrels in your attic," he had yelled at her.

She isn't going to pay the rent. She's heard the noise twice more since the phone call. He'll just have to get a ladder and take a look. She's resolved that she'll call him once a week about it. Three weeks and she hasn't called.

Her sister Maddy is on her phone-calling jag again. Maybe that's the reason. It's hard to come home from a day of doctor complaints, critically ill patients and over-anxious relatives to have to begin right in with Maddy. But of course she'll do it for her sister, whatever she has to do.

"Karen, I'm making this really nice dinner tonight. Let me tell you about it. You can come over."

She'll let Maddy go on about it—casseroles or some stuffed fish thing. Karen can sit and take off her clogs, begin cleaning them for the next day. Or she can walk up and down the tiles of the kitchen, trying to get the kinks out of her legs from all the standing. Sometimes she just collapses in a chair and Maddy rambles.

Her sister has gone through all the stages in the last

two years. Karen knows the signs from watching her patients in the ICU, from helping to tell their relatives that this one just isn't going to make it. Maddy's stages are longer and more pronounced than anything Karen has ever dealt with. She feels helpless in the face of it. Maddy is barely making it; her husband, Tim, is lost in his job. It reminds Karen of a snowfall that will never melt, a thundering load of ice and cold that fell on them one day and lodged in their bones, their muscle tissue, the pulsing wanderings of their veins. A storm still rages inside all of them.

Maddy pauses and Karen talks to her about a funny experience with a patient. She is careful in what she says. She rarely deals with children and stays away from stories about them. Maddy listens. And then she talks about Tim, relating an argument they had over a memory. It is, of course, about Jessy. Karen has to help out. What color dress did they give her for Easter three years ago? Karen leans on the counter. There is not one fresh flower left in the bunch, those tiny carnations they sell on the street corners hoping you'll think you're buying spring or happiness or love. Karen grabs the vase and turns it upside down into the sink.

"Pink," she says angrily. And then tries to change her voice or change something. "Maddy, let's go shopping on Saturday. I need some scrubs for spring. All the new stuff is coming out. It's getting time for you to buy jeans and tops. You're going to go camping again now, aren't you—you and Tim?"

"The trial."

"It's coming and that's good. But you'll need to get away on the weekends."

"When it's over I'm moving, Karen, I'm leaving here forever."

"Yes, I know. But think of Tim." Today Karen

doesn't say any more; it feels like it's almost over. Maddy is sounding tired. Karen always wonders what Maddy does after she hangs up the phone, but she hasn't the strength to ask her.

She can't help but think about Jessy after the call. Maddy must. All the time? Karen can't get inside her sister's head, but then is there anything in medicine or psychology that could heal her? Jessy's been dead a little over two years. Maddy's phone call sprees usually start up after the anniversary: October. Since then they've marked their lives in stages. Praying to find the murderers. Praying for the best prosecutors. Now aching for it all to be over. And forever—but October. A day that first filled Karen with awe, a glassy blue sky, a red euonymus bush dropping leaves around her shoes. The green gash of the tiny lawn, a moon already hanging, full—but then the cold air coming down on all of them.

Karen finds she is staring into the sink. She cleans up the flowers. She washes the smelly green slime away with streams of cold water. The phone begins to ring again.

"Karen, I hate bothering you. It's Tim."

"It's okay."

"Maddy call you today?"

"Yes. She—"

"She okay? How did she sound?"

"About the same. Why?"

"I didn't think she'd tell you."

"Tell me what?"

"They've postponed the trial for another month."

"Fuck them all."

"The attorneys have good reason, but Maddy—"

"She'll just have to make it, Tim. I think she will."

"I wish she'd get angry again. She can function best when she's ready to fight."

"She hasn't given up. I think I can tell that. She's not doing that funny thing with her voice. She's not playing some role. Remember when I told you I thought she might be different people, she sounded so different when she'd call? But she's out of that. She's herself. She just keeps remembering. I mean she doesn't talk about it much, but she's still going over it and over it, and—"

"Okay."

Karen hears impatience or more. "I'm sorry."

"She'll always go over it—her whole life. We both will. How can we go one day without saying if only, if only we didn't leave her alone. If only we had stayed home with her, if only. I'm sorry. Listen to us. Listen to me. God."

"Anything you want me to do?"

"No. We'll see you on Friday. Dinner at seven, right?"

"Sure. See you."

Karen walks away from his voice, from the ritual of their lives. She opens the refrigerator, pauses, and then closes it. She walks into a small TV room and tugs on the drape cord letting in the last frail light of the day. The cassette is already in the machine. She pushes PLAY and hears Maddy's voice, her shoes walking across the kitchen floor, Jessy laughing in the background. "Apple," Jessy says like "awpell." "Cat," Jessy says, dragging out the "t" sound. Maddy's shoes on the floor. "Eat your cookie, Jessy." "Cook, cook," Jessy says. Karen snaps off the tape. She pulls the cassette out of the machine and hurls it against the far wall. Then she rushes over to pick it up, put it carefully back on the shelf.

Maddy once said that it helps to think that Jessy is two years older now. She's not eight, she's ten and she understands what happened to her and the terror of it has subsided. Karen decided a year ago, though she never brought it up with Maddy, she never wants to ever bring it up, that Jessy was unconscious almost immediately; they beat her and raped her and she didn't know anything. Karen had decided.

In the bathroom upstairs, she turns on the radio and begins to wash her hair. She has to listen to music, the weather, the news. She dries her hair. She combs it. There is this commercial on with a woman's voice, an obnoxious voice, a voice that Karen thinks sounds like Cool Whip or frozen French toast or, no, actually a soggy piece of thawed French toast—all sticky and gooey. She is going on and on about perfume and men and Karen turns it off. And then she hears it again, something on the roof. Something slaps and knocks at the roof tiles, something that doesn't really scamper like a squirrel, something that keeps it up for the longest time, wanting to get in away from the snow and the cold.

On the Cusp

"No. I absolutely will not wear patent leather," Carrie says sliding along the thick carpet of the store in a pair of bright cherry-red shoes. Kate frowns at the color, more appropriate for a disco dancer. "And I won't have straps this time, Mom. Straps are for wimps." She says this executing another slide and knocking over three boxes of shoes that the lady across from them is trying on.

"Oops!"

Kate waits, but there is no apology from her daughter who slides away again, arms flung out, head bent to watch the shoes. "Come over here please."

Carrie looks back over her shoulder, Kate's frown only producing a large grin. "I'm skating, Mom. See? Or even better, I can twirl and be a dancer, just like you."

Kate resigns herself. This trip to the store allows her to sit down after a day of car pools, helping out at Carrie's Brownie meeting and addressing 500 envelopes for the fund-raiser at Carrie's school. Let the child knock over all the boxes in the store; let her do what she wants for the six minutes it takes the saleswoman to dig for leather shoes without straps, size 2.

More and more it's easier to let Carrie call the shots. Eight-year-olds! Independent thinkers. Chaos creators. These descriptions float around in Kate's head as she tries to find things in Carrie's closet or sort through piles of school papers, chapter books and junk toys from various Happy Meals. The little girl who had wandered after Kate with her play broom imitating *Mommy* has been swallowed up by a charmer who lately sees things only one way—hers. Kate may worry about this. But on those evenings when Dan has brought home a briefcase of work and Carrie wants help with math or is insisting on their combative and continuous Monopoly game, Kate quietly reminds him that Carrie's moods are part of normal development. Dan agrees: "That's the deal, Kate, the hard part is getting *you* to admit it."

"I know what's going on. I'm not asleep at the switch." But that night the conversation ended there, Dan being preoccupied with something—often his standard response. And Kate didn't bother to demand his attention, relate that for her, accepting change in her only child—or change in general—is just plain difficult.

Driving home from the shoe store, Carrie sits in the front seat, hands neatly folded in her lap. Kate smiles at such lady-like posture and the compromise purchase in the box at her daughter's feet—quiet looking blue leather shoes, with tiny grosgrain bows, no straps. The shoes of a little girl slowly growing up.

"What sign am I?" Carrie asks, turning from the window and punching the radio buttons.

"Sign? Astrological sign?" Kate asks her.

"I think so. Jenny Armor says that she's Sage-a-taurus or something."

"Sagittarius. She's talking about astrology, a system developed thousands of years ago to link the stars at the time of your birth with the kind of person you are or will be. If Jenny Armor is a Sagittarius I'm pretty sure her birthday would be November or December."

"Well what sign am I?"

"I'm not sure. I'd have to check a chart. There's usually one in the newspaper, but it hardly means anything, Care. The stars don't affect your life choices or behavior. It's how you grow up, what you learn in school, and how your parents raise you. All of that helps determine what choices you'll make and who you'll become."

Carrie turns up the volume of the radio. A raucous beat and bleating male voice fill the car. She giggles.

"Jenny Armor sings this on the playground."

"God help her mother," Kate says turning the volume way down.

"Now I'm all set for dress-up day next Thursday," Carrie says. "No yucky uniform for one whole day—my new blue shoes, my yellow skirt and the blouse with the pink flowers."

"You'll look like a rainbow."

"It all goes together, Mom, you said."

"Just kidding."

As Kate pulls into their driveway, the radio is now playing an older, softer rock tune and Carrie immediately turns it up. For a moment Kate is back, a room full of eager women watching her execute her choreographed movements, every turn and twist, every step and jump in sync with the music—all of it still there, a film playing in her head, her body eager to do what it still knows so well. She snaps off the radio.

"Care, when we go in, please set the table for dinner and put your shoes in your closet—okay? Dress-up day is coming, but I don't want to be tripping over your shoes between then and now."

"I wonder what sign Patrick Porter is. Jenny said that Patrick is the same sign she is. Jenny's weird."

"Carrie, you haven't heard a word." And Kate slowly repeats Carrie's instructions with love in her voice.

"What's a lactating woman?" Carrie asks a few days later at breakfast. Kate is standing at the kitchen window staring out at the purple plum tree and willing it into bloom. She turns, laughs. "Where did you come up with that question?"

"It's right here on your vitamin bottle," Carrie mumbles through a mouthful of French toast. She is hurrying through breakfast so as not to miss her ride.

"It's a woman who is nursing her baby. When I had you I started taking vitamins and I never stopped. You take as much out of me now as you did then."

"Aw, Mom."

"You're my one and only Chunk of Love."

"I'm no longer a chunk. But…oops, Mom! I forgot. Jenny Armor asked me to stay over Friday night."

"I thought Jenny was weird."

"She is. But I like her. She's my best friend at school. And Karen, Merle and Mary will be there to."

"A slumber party," Kate says. "Don't you remember your father is going to a work session in Los Angeles, so he'll be gone for the entire weekend and I planned lots for you and me to do. We were—"

"We can still do some of that stuff."

Kate knows Dan would let Carrie go. They have argued about the proper time for Carrie to start "leaving the nest" periodically, but Dan has eight sisters and when Kate tries to pin him down as to when *they* had permission to start dating etcetera, he laughs and says since they were two.

"Okay. I'll call Jenny's Mom. But I'd really like you home around noon on Saturday. You might need a nap and then we could go to the movies."

Carrie's response to this cool offer is to dig a scrap of paper from her backpack. "A quar-i-us. Patrick Porter is A quar-i-us. What sign am I Mom? Will you *please* find out for me before I go to Jenny's?"

"Whoops, Care, let's go, your ride's here. You've got your backpack. Did you remember your dues for the Brownie meeting?" And Carrie is finally out the door.

As Kate stands in the doorway waving and feeling pleased that it's not her day to drive, she sees a woman running up the street—a bright flash in a purple running suit. Watching, Kate wraps her bathrobe more tightly around her, then slowly closes the door as the woman disappears. Her own running shoes are jammed somewhere in the back of her closet, probably next to her taps, character shoes and last pair of ballet slippers thrown into a box after her injury—all gathering dust.

She attacks the dishes, starts the laundry, and then sits momentarily to scan today's list: *call furnace repairman, bake for Brownie meeting, set up dentist appointments, pick up cleaning, go to post office—overnight envelopes for Dan, inflate tire on Carrie's bike.* Okay. She hesitates. Then flipping to a blank sheet she writes: *call physical therapist.*

Stacking the paper, pencils and books that Carrie has scattered all over the kitchen table, Kate walks to the bookcase in the family room to put them away, only to see a familiar-looking box shoved next to a jumble of workbooks and paper odds and ends. Inside are Carrie's new shoes still wrapped in fragile tissue paper having never made it to Carrie's closet. Kate is vaguely angry. Carrie only hears what she wants to hear and Kate will have to teach her more about follow-through. She leaves the shoes where they are.

On Friday evening, Carrie leaves at six. She wears her gold heart and chain after begging permission from Kate and arguing that this overnight is a special occasion.

"You're right, Carrie, but if you need anything, have Mrs. Armor call me."

Later Dan phones from the Hilton in LA.

"Mark changed his schedule, he's here and that will help the presentation. But I should have urged you to come. There's so much theatre and dance here we could have squeezed in a show."

Though she hungers to know, Kate doesn't ask who's performing. She ends the call with a good luck wish, forgetting to remind him that Carrie is at her very first slumber party. The salad she makes is boring and she begins to think about buttered popcorn and calling Joan who loves French films. There's a new one at the Varsity and it's not too late to catch the 9:00 o'clock. But by the phone taped to the wall is a piece of notebook paper with a scrawled message: *Mom, plez find out what sign I am. Member? Carrie*

Follow-through. Maybe lack of one is a family trait.

Kate goes down into the basement where she keeps file folders of stuff she might need someday: how to unclog the garbage disposal, recipes for a Hawaiian luau and numbers to call for the repair of screens, bicycles and various household machines. There is also a stack of old magazines and in minutes she finds it—a column about astrology that keeps readers up-to-date on their horoscopes. She locates Carrie's May 20th birthday. Carrie is on the cusp, her birthday landing between Taurus and Gemini, she supposedly having a little of both signs. Kate reads and smiles: *Taurus people are often lazy unless the goal or task is one that suits them. Gemini people embrace the world and want to be helpful.* Maybe sharing this information is a good thing. Maybe the silly horoscope will encourage Carrie to work on her positive traits. Again, follow-through.

But then Kate sees it, the bright orange folder with ragged edges. She knows what's inside: sheets explaining the exercises she is to do to strengthen her stretched and often painful posterior tibial tendon—four pages of illustrated movements with a suggested number of repetitions. The folder shouts that she has given up, rarely wearing her arch supports and avoiding activities that might increase her discomfort as she slowly evolves into a couch potato. Opening it, there is a note from the physical therapist dated two years ago. It is written on an angle across the page in large bold script: *Exercise every day—see sheets; shoe arch supports every day; ballet? you're done; dance exercise? possibly on limited basis. Call for appointment in six months. Will re-evaluate.*

Later, Kate flips through the photo album that Dan keeps on his bedside table—Carrie's life in pictures. Periodically updated, there are recent photos of Carrie at her eighth birthday party, roller-skating, singing at the school Christmas concert, and Carrie at her ballet recital.

For awhile, Kate stares at this last one, avoiding picking up the book she's been reading—*The Last Dance,* a memoir about a ballet dancer who trained under George Balanchine. Rising slowly from the bed, she reaches her arms over her head in the fifth position, slowly adjusting her feet. *Ballet? You're done.*

She knows where they are. After getting her newest pair of athletic shoes from the closet, she slips in her arch supports. They still fit just fine. Okay.

Much later, when Kate turns out the light, she has organized a pile of reading materials—*The Last Dance*, and other texts about ballet, choreography and jazz dance, as well as the orange folder and a well-worn pamphlet from the city college, folded to the page listing classes for dance teachers. She immediately falls asleep.

Saturday afternoon Carrie is overflowing with stories about Jenny's house, the food they ate, the games they played and a description of both Merle and Karen's backpacks. Between yawns, she shows Kate a picture she drew and the Happy Meal Cinderella fan she is going to keep.

Kate shows Carrie the astrology table. "They call your birthday *being on the cusp*. It you want to believe any of it, it means you have some of the qualities of both signs—like you're at a turning point, going from one sign to the next."

"But what qualities do I have?"

"Supposedly as a Taurus you tend to be lazy and only work hard at the things you really like to do."

"Sounds like me," Carrie says earnestly.

"As a Gemini you want to be helpful to everyone."

" I like that."

"But Carrie all of this is just like a game. Stars won't make things work out for you. You've got to make your own life happen."

"Okay, I guess."

"You have to be responsible, Carrie, and remember to do things—like putting your new shoes away."

Carrie's huge blue eyes get even bigger.

"I put them—yeah, I didn't put them where you said. Gotta work on that."

"I'm sorry, Mrs. Michels, the schedule is full today," the physical therapist's receptionist tells Kate Monday morning. "But let's see…your chart indicates you haven't been in for a while. Another evaluation will be needed…Posterior tibial tendon, right foot. Have you been keeping up your strengthening exercises?"

"No."

"Are you still having pain?"

"Off and on."

"I can fit you in tomorrow, 10:00 a.m. And bring your shoe inserts. We'll have to see if those are still providing enough support."

Now Kate opens the orange folder often and begins. While exercising she sometimes reflects on the changes she is seeing in her daughter—Monday morning Carrie was standing at the door with her backpack and lunch when her ride pulled up. Monday night she presented Dan and Kate with a folder of papers from school—all A's and B's.

Tuesday she did dawdle over her breakfast and Kate had to help her find a homework assignment. But she remembered all the materials for the patch she was working on at Brownies and she even set the table without being asked. Wednesday was another good day, Carrie helping Kate with the grocery shopping and putting all of the canned goods and paper products away.

Thursday Kate has the car pool. Things are going

well, even though Carrie has lots of snarls in her hair and fidgets while Kate struggles to get them out. She does find her missing gym shoes and the last clean pair of navy socks that she has to wear with her uniform. The phone rings twice—Joan's children are sick and won't need a ride and Mary has a very early dental appointment. Fine, more time for Kate and Carrie to linger over breakfast chatting and enjoying the morning. They leave for school with enough time to arrive before the first bell rings.

As they drive the familiar streets, Carrie explains details of the art project she has completed and the number of chapter books she can add to her Reading List. Kate smiles to herself—her parental guidance is truly having positive effects.

But as they pull into the parking lot of the school, something feels wrong. Then Carrie is noticing too. It is dress-up day. All the children are gathering on the steps in pastel skirts, bright-colored slacks or new spring sweaters. Carrie stares at her hands folded tightly on the skirt of her plaid uniform.

"Mom, you should have—" but she stops abruptly. Kate waits. Finally Carrie says quietly, "I forgot."

Kate hands clutch the steering wheel; they could drive home and hurry back and just be a little late.

"I guess it's because I'm on that—what's it called—cusp."

Kate leans over and gently encircles her daughter's thin shoulders.

"It's not because you're on the cusp, Care, it's that you're growing up and growing up is one of the hardest things we have to do."

"Mom," Carrie says suddenly, "I have to hurry."

Kate reaches out and straightens the heart on Carrie's chain, making sure that it is in the right place.

Carrie gets out of the car and runs, her thin legs flashing in the sunlight. Though she's close to being late, she can't resist jumping over a short wall of flagstone before she climbs the school steps.

Kate doesn't drive home. Instead, she heads to the city college to sign up for the Level One class in Choreography and to look at the dance-exercise class schedule.

"Kate, let's schedule you for a series of PT appointments," the physical therapist said on Tuesday. "We have to rule out ballet, but we can strengthen your healthy tendons to help support the weak one. As for teaching dance-exercise, I think you'll be able to. You'll wear a softer athletic shoe made for this purpose and your arch supports of course. When we both agree you're ready, I would teach only one class to start. And make it low-impact. You'll find students who need the exact same thing."

When a week ago, Dan asked Kate why she was again wearing athletic shoes, she reminded him of her injury.

"I think it's great you're back in action, Kate, and taking care of yourself. And you know I love seeing you sweat."

Their laughter finally drifted to a more serious talk about Carrie, her life and all the discoveries and choices spread out before her.

"Her life is just limitless compared to ours. But we've got that wisdom thing to help us adjust."

"To change, right?" Kate said.

And she almost mentioned follow-through, because like Carrie, Kate is also at a turning point. Maybe it's time for her to check out her astrological sign.

Angel Hair

The coffee gathering at Liz Grimm's house was the first time anyone had been out in the small New England town of Hamilton since Pia Piper was fired from the local preschool. Accused of fondling a boy-child in her classroom, Piper had instantly proclaimed her innocence and left the school weeping. Later she sent a missive to the school board stating that possibly someone, she didn't know who, had wanted to do her harm and helped set the entire lie in motion. "*If I lose my ability to teach,*" she wrote, "*I will extract a payment from all of you. Believe me.*"

The Hamilton newspaper devoted a major headline and column to the story once a week. It regurgitated the same information, which continued to be sketchy and didn't prove anything. A photograph of Piper wearing the only garment she seemed to own—a very long sweater, color blocked in yellow and red—accompanied each story along with the words she had used to exonerate herself: *I was ill the day this child made up such a story. I was not even there. I am innocent.*

Her claim only fueled the gossip that spread through the town like a plague. Members of the preschool staff, every parent and even religious and political leaders endlessly debated her statements. Of course the child's testimony was shielded—only lawyers and counselors having access, and only they knowing which child had claimed the harm.

One mother, Angela Holcomb, went to the coffee, hoping that such a shock to the community would have toned down Liz Grimm's familiar rants. Single, with no children, Liz felt it her civic duty to hunt out the details of any problem that occurred in Hamilton. After forming a strong opinion regarding the latest crisis, she would summon the town's mothers to her home to warn them of the dangers connected to the issue. In truth, she merely added to their already busy and stressful lives, while brazenly conveying that nothing could touch or unsettle her.

As Angela helped her toddler, Susan, from the car, she decided that Liz would just proclaim Pia Piper guilty, thus making it impossible for the teacher to have a fair hearing or to ever work again. Such thoughts made her hesitate—why even bother to go inside.

"Mommy, look," Susan said as thunder began to sound over their heads. A cardinal, like a scarlet fireball, fluttered there, right over Liz's front door.

Inside, while greeting the women in a circle in the living room, Angela began to feel some relief and vague hope for an atmosphere of consolation and healing. Her five-year-old son, Jeff, attended the preschool and to a one, each woman gathered there also had a child at the school.

They had to know firsthand how loving and engaging Piper really was—how she shared her skills with musical instruments with the children and wrote poems to celebrate special school occasions. She was clever and fearless when it came to cleaning up after a vomiting child or one that had soiled pants or was bleeding from somewhere. And since her arrival the school no longer needed to pay for pest control. Angela had witnessed the small-boned woman wrestling a bat from the ceiling with the flick of a towel. But she couldn't figure out how Pia had irrevocably dealt with the rodents that for decades lived under the floor at the back of the preschool. Surely, these women were aware of Pia's amazing skills.

But as rain dripped down the stained glass window behind her, Liz fumed about the situation with Piper and then brought up other fear-laden concerns: the increasing number of outsiders moving into Hamilton and the subsequent rise in crime. She drew vivid pictures of various dangers, linking all to cultural negligence and the crumbling of social mores. Looking around the room, she tried to whip everyone into a frenzy, focusing on one mother and then another, her eyes almost shouting *take a position, take a side.*

"We are all guilty of tearing down our society, Ladies. And though each one of you may not be accused of touching a child improperly, you have yelled inappropriately at a child, yours or someone else's. You have lied about something, kept money that wasn't yours, cheated on your taxes, gone through a red light, gossiped about your neighbors and—" She stopped to sip at her coffee.

Angela broke in, almost shouting: "This isn't helping, Liz. Can't we talk about something else? Sure I ache for the parents of that child. But Pia Piper deserves a fair hearing. Can't we talk about something ordinary right now, like summer plans for the children or that we need to replace the worn carpet at the preschool?"

Her words elicited only silence, all the mothers

turning their heads to stare at her. Then way back in the corner, Lauren DiBolt finished wiping a crumb of blueberry muffin from the corner of her mouth and began to speak: "Piper's as guilty as sin, Angela. We all know it. She's an evil person and should never have been allowed to have anything to do with our innocent children. You can't be on the fence about these things. You have to rat her out. So take a side about the bitch, Angela, and take it now."

Such a word! Angela thought of Susan, but a quick look confirmed the child was happily playing in a far corner. So she had to speak, and now, even though her hands were suddenly icy despite the hot cup of coffee she was holding. "Did I say something wrong? I only want to be happy again, not get up every day worrying about Jeff, about all the children."

Lauren DiBolt raised her left arm and pointed at Angela. "Everyone here can listen to Liz, yes. But each one of you has to make your own decision. Commit and stick. Piper is an outsider, not one of us. I'm voting we ride Piper out of Hamilton, the sooner the better. She should be spurned from teaching innocents forever."

There was a pause, only the sound of coffee cups hitting saucers broke the quiet. Angela wondered whether it was Liz or Lauren that had silenced all of these women, put them in a kind of trance. Or was it she, Angela?

Lauren kept up her rant. "Well, what side are you going to break on, Angela, and you too Liz? You afraid to speak up?"

Now Angela's whole body rippled with chill. This was not a room for consolation and healing. Her hands shook as she set down her coffee and rose to grab Susan from the clutch of other toddlers.

"Angela?" Lauren's voice again. "Speak up."

Hugging her daughter to her chest, Angela looked around the room of faces, then blurted out: "I don't know. But—well, the child—I guess she must be guilty." And then turning toward the door, she escaped.

Later that same day, Angela's husband Jacob came home from an extended business trip. The rain had cleared and the temperatures leapt to an unbelievable 75 degrees. So he drove his family to the ocean.

He ran with Jeff and Susan along the water's edge while Angela sat on the beach wrapped in a towel, her eyes blurring with the sun on water. She tried not to think of Liz's coffee, the brashness of Lauren DiBolt and the stupefied looks of the other women. She wondered how the child who was the focus of the investigation was doing. How horrible for him to be plunged into a world that was foreign and scary for adults—not to mention children.

Then the loudspeakers began to fill the beach with an announcement—a child named Tamerina was missing. Angela tried to blot out her own children's happy shouts and the sloshing of the water on the beach so she could hear.

Tamerina, Five years old. Wearing a green bathing suit with an orange flower sewn on the front. Tamerina. If you find her bring her to the refreshment stand.

"*Tamerina, Tamerina, have you seen her?*" The words pumped through Angela's head to some shred of melody.

They stayed at the beach for three hours, Angela glued to the towel, listening. When Jacob said he was tired and it was time to dry off the children, Angela rose, wobbling, stumbling.

"You okay?" Jacob asked.

"Oh. The sun," Angela said, reaching back down and pulling a clean towel from her beach bag.

The children ate snacks and then started to quarrel over the sand buckets as the loudspeaker continued the message about Tamerina. Angela told Jacob she wanted to stay. Could he please go to the refreshment stand and buy burgers for dinner? He argued for leaving—the children had enough sun this early in the season.

"But the missing child."

"I'm sure they'll find that kid."

"And then there was this meeting."

"What meeting? Do you have some meeting to-night?"

She looked up at him, wondering what it was like not to worry about Pia Piper every single day. Their discussion on the subject had been brief and he had never mentioned it again. He was so wrapped up in his tax work with April 15th looming. But a supposedly traumatized preschooler and now this missing child in a bathing suit—that warranted attention. And Angela couldn't leave the beach thinking that maybe she, her whole family, should be searching for the missing Tamerina.

Jacob stood above her. "Could you focus here. The kids. They're eager to go now. Okay?"

Yes. Her attention was elsewhere, but she nodded, then rose, her feet like lead, her hands unable to fold towels or gather toys with any sense of speed. Jacob turned back to look at her, raising his eyebrows.

And then the loud speaker came on again. Tamerina was found. Her mother was to come and get her. Quickly, Angela gathered up the last of their things and walked away, fiercely hugging the beach bag to her chest and watching the indentations of her children's feet ahead of her in the warm sand.

A fine mist of rain was falling on Monday as Angela and Susan hurried into the Hamilton Preschool to pick up Jeff. They huddled in the hallway with the other mothers as the replacement for Pia and the regular teacher finished up Mark DiBolt's fifth birthday party. First Lauren DiBolt came out, bearing an empty cake pan.

"Mark's in another world today. I'll have to tie him to a tree to get anything done before bedtime."

Angela squeezed Susan. Lauren raked frosting away from the sides of the cake pan and licked it off her fingers. Then the children exploded from the room wearing blue and orange construction paper birthday crowns and clutching candy bags that dripped with pieces of macaroni, colored sequins and lots of glue.

When Angela spotted Jeff, she reached for him, getting a firm hold on his collar so she could propel him toward the door. Even so, Jeff managed to wriggle away from her and run out into the rain.

In the car he talked incessantly about the party, then asked her *When is **my** birthday? Dad said soon. What cake are you going to make for me? What candy can we get? Can we get Skittles instead of M&M's?*

Angela answered by repeatedly telling him to put on his seatbelt. When he finally did, he spent the rest of the drive teasing Susan about being too small to go without a car seat. Angela didn't stop him, mesmerized by the sound of his voice, his enthusiasm pushing his vocal range upwards to soprano, a pause for a breath crashing it back down to tenor.

On Friday morning, Jeff had a sore throat and Angela kept him home from preschool. There was a flu going around, rumored to hang on for weeks. Angela would stop her ironing to check Jeff for fever, gently pushing his hair back to kiss his forehead. Then the phone would ring or the dryer would buzz and she would turn on the television for him and Susan. But a battle soon began because Jeff kept turning the channel to watch the news—Angela seeing the familiar photograph of Pia Piper on the screen.

"Turn that off, Jeffrey," she would say, cupping the telephone receiver with her hand or balancing a basket of laundry on her hip, "that's not for children. Be good now."

Once Jeff said outright, "I like Miss Piper. She plays really cool music and she lets me use lots of glue."

Around noon Liz Grimm called. Remembering the coffee gathering, Angela decided to keep the call brief. She didn't like that Liz made her feel insignificant and uninformed.

"I have news. Mark DiBolt is missing. He disappeared yesterday on his fifth birthday. They have no clues, nothing."

Angela tangled fingers in her hair and began to pace. "Are you absolutely sure, Liz? I mean where did you hear this and are they asking for volunteers to go search for him? Will his picture be in the newspapers?"

"That's all I know. As a favor I'm calling everyone."

"A favor? This devastating news! And again, who told you?"

"Why everyone is talking about it. And that only makes sense."

"None of it makes sense. Maybe he went to a relative's house or fell down a window well. There has to be some mistake. You bring up all these horrible problems, but you never have any solutions."

"Listen to me, Angela, we voted after you left the coffee. You, Lauren and Sarah Brady were the only ones who were sure Piper's guilty. The only ones."

"I'm not sure. Did I say I was sure? I really haven't taken the time to read about it, think it through. Who can with a part-time job, two young children and a husband who travels? Where is Piper now?" Angela felt panicked.

"How do you not know what's going on, Angela. They didn't charge her with anything, but they did tell her to leave town."

"When. Why did they do that?"

"I guess the child was mistaken. Some of the psychological testing was inconclusive. In the end, I was right. Again."

"But then why make Pia Piper leave town?"

"Well, gotta go," and Liz hung up.

Angela stood listening to the dial tone, tears welling in her eyes, her body colder than cold. She found Susan and Jeff on the floor in the family room, their bodies limber but distorted in the lens of her tears.

That evening Jacob had to catch a flight to help a major client far away in Oregon. Angela lay awake, listening to the quiet. She wanted the phone to ring saying Mark was found, that it was over and everything was simply a mistake. Around five in the morning all the dogs in the neighborhood seemed to bark at once, their sound a rising crescendo and then abruptly—silence. Angela sat bolt upright in bed. She listened for the movements of her children down the hall—Jeff's cough, Susan's turnings. When she finally lay back down and fell asleep, she dreamed she spoke with Pia Piper. The teacher stopped her on a road outside of town, asked her to describe Mark, but all Angela could remember about the child was that he had light, blond hair, glints of gold, fiery glints, angel hair.

Over the weekend, the community of Hamilton seemed suspended in time. Preschool was cancelled for the coming week. People slogged through their routines so that they could go home, lock the door and clutch each other tightly. Pictures of Pia Piper and Mark DiBolt continued to pop up everywhere, and though Angela told herself there was nothing to fear, she stayed inside with the children.

At first she moved quickly, scrubbing cabinets and looking into closets, keeping the radio on for news of Mark, the phone near her at all times. But after awhile, she found herself staring out the window into the back garden—no one was there. The tulips had popped in the unseasonably warm weather; they blazed fiery red and searing yellow. She thought she saw honeybees buzzing around them and the words to an old poem circled in her head, "*And honeybees had lost their stings.*" But the children didn't come to the window with her and they didn't ask to go outside.

She wondered if somehow Jeff knew about Mark's missing and had told Susan. But she didn't say anything, not wanting to frighten her children. Maybe when Jacob came home they would sit down as a family and discuss the situation. But Jacob called saying he had to stay longer, everything had to be dealt with before April 15th.

"Keep Jeff home till he's completely well. And get a babysitter when you need to work. Or call off. I'll check in when I can."

When the call ended, Angela realized they hadn't talked about Mark—Jacob hadn't asked for an update or shown any concern for this missing child. And when she called her supervisor, she found herself lying, telling him that she had the flu. Going to bed that night she remembered Liz's words: *We are all guilty of tearing down the society we live in. You have all lied about something...*

When Mark had been missing for almost a week, Angela noticed that Jeff was ignoring his toys, not fooling around with the TV. Instead he spent all of his time with Susan. Even their voices were different. Where once they were riotous and crazy and Angela couldn't wait for their bedtimes, now they seemed quieter, fading in the bright sunlight of the family room. It made Angela slow her pace, listening for what they would say. She floated thickly as if through deep waters, arms outstretched, heart open; and Jeff and Susan bobbed away from her into their own child-world. So she cut herself off from the world outside, not even thinking to call her pediatrician for advice, or to call Liz who surely would have the freshest news.

Then one night while Jeff was swallowing some cough medicine, he looked at her intently and said: "I know Mark isn't coming back to my school." Angela stammered, agreeing that yes Mark was missing, but he would be found very soon and everything would be okay. Jeff merely eased his shoulders from her grasp and slipped away as if his entire body was expelling a huge sigh.

The next morning he lay very still in his bed, looking up at her. She reached for the thermometer, but he pushed it away.

"In my dream there was a big hole, in the side of a mountain. And I wasn't sure what to do."

"Was it a bad dream?"

"No. I think there was candy inside, or a pony to ride. But I didn't want to leave you."

"Let's take your temp," Angela insisted leaning over to hold him, his body light and cool. He smiled up at her.

"Okay, you're not sick, school is open, so you can go back today."

"Great!" Jeff shouted and Angela felt his body fill with energy as he wriggled to get free of her hug. Standing by his dresser, he reached up to open the top drawer and rifle through its contents, too short in stature to really see what he was doing.

"Jeff, stop now. Listen to me, "Angela said. "Be careful today, okay? Stay by your teachers." When he turned around smiling, he waved the shirt he had found, a striped red and yellow one with the bold head of Mickey Mouse across the front.

At the preschool, Angela cradled Susan on her hip as she stared at the Birthday Bulletin Board. There was Mark's name—still encircled with the gold birthday crown. Jeff's birthday was ten days away. Should she go ahead, have a party in this classroom with Lauren and Mark DiBolt not there? But shouldn't she attempt to make life feel normal for the children? And though Liz Grimm accused her of being uninformed, just knowing everything in the news—scandals, wars, the lies of powerful men—that wouldn't help her raise Susan and Jeff. Being with them, reading and playing with them, showing them good example—now that would mold her children into good people.

"Angela!" Sarah Brady was tugging on her sleeve. "You did good siding with me and DiBolt about that Piper woman."

Angela stared at this woman whose crown of thick braided hair framed a face placid and devoid of emotion. "But Mark," Angela whispered.

"Well, yeah. But DiBolt never could keep track of her kid."

Angela's voice caught: "I'm taking it back, what I said. Lauren put me on the spot. I should never have said what I did—I needed much more information to make such a judgment."

"Aw, Angela, you do go on. Stick with me. What if they rehire that sick sick piece of —, what then?"

But the question went unanswered as Jeff ran up, announcing that Patrick Brady's birthday party was the next day. When he looked at Sarah Brady and asked if they were *really* going to have chocolate cake, Angela wanted to cover his mouth with her hand. Instead she patted his head.

Driving, Angela found herself searching for something out the car windows—the form of a boy like Mark that might suddenly appear; a signpost rearing up with information or guidance, something she needed to know. But eventually her fingers trailed over to the radio and she turned it on, the car filling with the delicate single notes of a flute that pulled them all forward, mesmerized them with its calming progression of lilting tones. Her searching floated away.

While Jeff attended Patrick Brady's birthday party at the preschool, Angela took Susan for a walk in the park. They touched blooming pussy willow branches and budding magnolias. Angela lifted the child from the

stroller to sniff and smell, study the birds circling overhead, the bees flitting through the blossoms.

"Bees, buzz, buzz," Susan said. Then they went for
Jeff.

Late that afternoon, Angela answered the phone. It
was Liz. "I know you are going to tell me more bad
news."

"Patrick Brady is missing—the afternoon of his
fifth birthday. And Pia Piper was supposed to report to
the police station when she moved to the next town,
but she never showed up."

Now Angela demanded that the children stay inside—but for the first time in weeks, Jeff begged to go
out. She tried to stay calm, explaining that it would only
be for a few days. But as she spoke, the words *lie, liar*
seemed to float across the kitchen wall.

When later in the week, one of the preschool
mothers invited Jeff over to play, Angela let him go.
After a shorter passage of time than occurred after
Mark's disappearance, the school reopened. When she
dropped off Jeff, Angela passed by the Birthday Bulletin Board. Jeff's day loomed.

She ignored her chores, spent hours scanning the
local newspaper and the New York City papers, but
there was no information about Pia Piper or Patrick or
Mark. She'd lost her job because of absences and maybe her lies. She tried to push aside worries, but they
haunted her. She even had dreams that circled back to
Liz's coffee. She would awake with a start, reliving Lauren DiBolt's words: *You have to rat her out. So take a side
about the bitch, Angela, and take it now.*

Once when Jacob called, they talked briefly of a
birthday gift for Jeff, and Jacob made a reference to the

night of their son's birth. A stream of those moments rushed back at her—the bumpy, slushy drive to the hospital, a spring snowstorm, wet flakes piling and sliding down the car windows...Jacob hung up on parking the car, letting a nurse push Angela through sliding doors into a delivery room...no time to wait for Jacob's return, for anything...precious few fiery seconds...and she all alone, pushing her firstborn son out into the world...so captivating, so powerful.

And then as Jacob rambled about some tax stats, Angela pulled out a chair to sit down, hearing nothing more from him, still lost in the snow-fog and mist of that amazing, alluring and yet frightening birth night.

When Jeff couldn't decide if he wanted a Spiderman or GI Joe theme for his preschool party, Angela suggested they postpone everything. "After a while you'll know exactly what you want. Then we can do it."

"Then school will be over," Jeff said.

When later he proclaimed he wanted a strawberry cake, she found herself yelling at him, pulling him to her by his wrists so that he fiercely fought to free himself.

"What about Mark and Patrick? How can we have a party? They were your friends. Don't you remember?"

"I'm only five," Jeff said.

Their eyes locked. Was she responsible for this person, this boy who seemed unable to mirror any kind of empathy? Then he smiled, not a grin, but a smile that came from deep within him. And it held her as he ran off.

When Susan and Angela went to buy the ingredients for Jeff's cake, there was Liz, also buying strawberries.

"A sure sign of spring," Liz said. "And asparagus. Look, the price is coming down." She flipped several bunches into her cart which was packed with food. Then as Angela watched, she laid a hand on Susan's head. Angela didn't want Liz touching her child, but she held a melon in her hands. It was round and cold. For a moment she feared she might drop it.

"There's a psychic working Patrick's case," Liz was saying. "It's a waste. But you know Sarah Brady, always been a wacko. And DiBolt? She's locked up in some hospital." Then Liz simply turned away from them, pushing her cart and calling over her shoulder, "All I can say is I'm extremely fortunate for voicing Piper's innocence. You have to stay on top of these things."

Angela saw Susan, saw strawberries in her cart. They could get out of the store.

The rest of the day she felt herself falling down some dark hole, her body cumbersome, no longer a part of her. She had to fight off the urge to crawl into bed and sleep. When the phone rang her heart jumped—but there was no one there and after hanging up she tried to get the falling feeling back so that she could pinpoint it, discover where it led. But it eluded her and time was running out. She went into the kitchen and made Jeff's birthday cake.

After the preschool party, Angela watched Jeff's every move. The day held soft warmth and wisps of a breeze. The three of them went out on the lawn with lunch and leftover cake. While her children ran in the grass, Angela sat and watched their hair catching the sunlight, their bodies moving up and down the planes of the yard like birds soaring and landing. They were both having fun.

But then in one of Jeff's runs down the lawn, she heard sounds, the soothing notes of a high piped bird-call, or the humming of bees wings, and she smelled the pungent fragrance of shorn grass or scattered rose petals and saw the flash of a yellow/red cloak engulfing the sunlight for a split-second to reveal a shadowy opening in the hedge at the end of the lawn. Then in a blinding light there was Jeff, that was all she could see, the strands of his hair and then his entire head, and his entire body becoming golden and brilliant.

And though momentarily blinded, Angela began to shout, her voice rising, filling the yards and the streets nearby: "I was wrong—you are not guilty and I tried to say so. But I didn't shout it out. The child is the liar. Was it Mark, Patrick? Was it Jeff? Children make things up. You are innocent. The town mistreated you. I'll stand by you and speak for you. Just please give him back."

But when the blinding light faded away, sunlight brushed the lawn and the trees and there was only Susan in the grass. Angela crashed around the yard, her arms thrown open to the sky, her eyes searching for the opening in the hedge. But nothing.

"Pia Pia Piper!" Her voice tore through the trees as if to rip leaves from branches, her throat raw but her words reaching far away. "You are innocent. Please give Jeff back to me. I was weak, I was wrong."

And she turned to catch the laughing Susan, hoping to hold on to the child as her own body shook with weeping. Hadn't she known? And though she could not possibly have prevented this retribution, why let power-lessness overtake her? She could have held on to him. She'd had the power to deliver him here, this boy-child with peace and beauty behind his eyes. Innocent then. And now? Was that the allure, the very same? Innocence and perfection, full sunlit days and caverns of candy, days void of evil, land without lies—had that taken him? For he wasn't far away—not gone down some lonely road and not hidden in some dark building, but returned to truth. Truth. And now lulled by the dulcet sounds of the flute, the birds, the buzzing bees.

Could a small New England town awaken? Would Jacob blame her, leave her? But she must loosen her tongue, risk the name calling and sneers, even the tearing accusation of insanity, risk everything or they would all be gone, Susan too—piped away down a dark tunnel and out into the brightness on the other side. The children would all be gone.

Pumpkins

That day was a Friday and she drove with the pumpkins in the back of the car. They were going on the front porch. Now, this year, there would be only two. Heather drew the faces on in black magic marker. Maybe she would look more carefully at Heather's pumpkin face this time. Children's art revealed things.

She zipped the car through sloshy puddles under the viaduct. The windshield wipers set a pace. The pumpkins rolled in the back. She had been thinking about him off and on all day since it was his birthday. Only last year they had both, for a joke, entered the date and year of his birth in a computer. It told them his birth occurred on a Thursday. She had liked that. Heather, too, was a Thursday's child. They all had far to go.

The traffic light was changing, running through the old cycle backwards—red to yellow to green. She worked the gears and hurried. Her mother-in-law was nervous about the dentist. It was crazy for her to be doing this, but she'd gotten into the habit. Keith worked. Who else would take her? And moments later, there was the straight brick apartment building, the yellow slanted lines in the lot.

"You know it's Keith's birthday?"

She nodded as Mrs. Oates climbed in, pressing her

body against the other bucket seat.

"Call him, Rachel, call him. He'd call you on your day, now wouldn't he?"

Rachel backed the car down the drive.

"What's that rattle, your car can't need repairing already, you just—"

"Pumpkins," Rachel said.

Mrs. Oates watched out the window. She shifted her body and filled the car with some cloying perfume. Rachel rolled down a window.

"Don't open that now, please. I can't afford to catch a cold. I'm going through all this pain right now, I don't need—" Her voice stopped. Rachel looked over and noticed that Mrs. Oates wore a new raincoat. Her mother-in-law wasn't a fat woman, but she made great pies and cakes and made them constantly. The raincoat was a juicy berry color and it plumped around her.

"I got him a lovely angora sweater for his birthday. It's a blend. But I spent a lot of money on it."

Rachel decided Keith would hate it. He would complain about the tiny angora hairs messing up his dark pants.

"It's hard getting to be my age," Mrs. Oates said. "You have trouble getting to the stores and then when you're there what do you buy your son? What? It was easy when he was little, but now?"

At the dentist's they sat together on an orange vinyl couch. Mrs. Oates folded her glasses into a case. She snapped the case and then unsnapped it. She touched Rachel's arm and told her about an exercise program that she watched. "The girls have these little tummies. You ought to do it, Rachel." Her breath was warm and sick. Rachel thought about the mints buried in her purse. She thought about exercise. She didn't need to lose weight, when you didn't eat much, that wasn't a problem.

The hygienist came for Mrs. Oates. She nodded for Rachel to follow. Root canal was somewhat serious in an older person with a heart condition. Rachel followed. She watched the berry-colored coat come off and she thought that cakes and pies were even worse for one's heart. But it wasn't her business. Not really. And yet when Mrs. Oates was settled in the chair and the dentist made Rachel look at the x-rays, look down into Mrs. Oates' mouth to confirm, it was her business. No one else's. She backed out of the room. She could still see Mrs. Oates' grey hair against the back of the chair. She walked. Keith was 39. Mid-life. Mid-life crazies. Mrs. Oates' hair, probably auburn, had spread out on a table, some delivery table somewhere, and then Mrs. Oates spread her legs and touched the roundness of her belly and used energy and will to push Keith out. Thirty-nine years ago. It was her business. Mrs. Oates a connection.

Rachel went and called Heather.

"Did you get them, Mommy?"

"Yes, two, one big and one medium sized. They're in the car. Did you get a lot of homework?"

"I'm doing it. When you get home, then can we?"

"Yes."

"I'm going to design my face on paper first."

"Don't spend too much time, Heather. Your homework."

"The other kids were asking why we do it this way. They like to cut theirs. Yuck—all those seeds."

"Heather, I'll be home by six, okay?"

"Just listen, I forgot to tell you. I want to draw this picture for Dad's birthday. I had a dream about it. The picture is me carrying a birthday cake, but it's not a cake, it's noodles—a noodle cake!"

"There must be some significance there."

"Oh Mom—it's just a dream. It doesn't have to mean anything. Bye now."

Rachel hung up, smiling. The little artist was always at work. Creativity clung to her like the fragile blonde fuzz that Rachel could see on Heather's legs and arms when they wrestled in the sunshine. But Heather's fingers didn't always move the way she wanted. Her fifth Christmas, five years ago, she had worked at the card table every day. Rachel watched. Some of it was clay, some playdough, some drawing, pasting, cutting. On Christmas everything went into a bag. During the gift passing, Keith got the first one—a playdough face with runny-black hair and bulging eyes. He started to laugh before Heather could tell him the sculpture was of him, her Dad. Everyone clamped down on the laughter, turned serious and began the compliments. But Heather knew. Later when Keith announced it was her turn to give again, she looked into her bag, looked for a long time and then raised her face that was pink with grief. "It's all garbage," she said quietly, fighting so hard for that control. "All garbage." Rachel still grieved, thinking about that moment—Heather's face quivering, tears moving down her cheeks, the adults having broken through the barrier, crashed into that perfect place she thought she inhabited.

"We were cruel, all of us," Rachel had told Keith.

"She'll get over it, Rachel, don't take it so hard."

The dentist's waiting room was empty. Even the receptionist was gone from her desk. Rachel sat listening to the music. It was the feathery kind that no one really wants to hear. All distinguishing features had been removed so that it was clean and sterile like the alcohol and cotton in the back rooms. When she tried hard enough Rachel could identify a song. Now an old McCartney tune about a "butter pie." Rachel heard the melody and worked to remember the lyrics. Then she saw their first house. Keith had painted all the rooms a light celery just for her. It wasn't a well-built house, but the rooms were airy and they made love without worrying about apartment neighbors, and they turned the radio up loud and sang and chased each other up and down the halls, laughing like children. There was no clutter around them then, they had almost no furniture. But in the second house, even though they filled up the rooms, Keith kept buying more and weighing down their life. There was little space for music, and none for any more children.

"Mrs. Oates?" Rachel heard the name and looked up for her mother-in-law. The old woman wasn't there. The hygienist stood in the doorway. Rachel thought she saw blood on her white pantsuit.

"She's okay, isn't she?" Rachel was standing.

"Yes, of course. The doctor just wants to discuss the post-op care with you. Follow me."

Mrs. Oates moaned all the way home. Rachel talked quietly to her, but after a while she had no energy for words. The rain still came down; the car radio talked about the end of Indian summer, the series of inevitable rainstorms. Rachel felt the words like pressure, a dark curtain descending. All she could see was this older neighborhood, the houses leaning toward the street, apartment buildings with cracked front stairs, older people moving along with little wire grocery carts.

"Here was are, Mom."

Rachel jumped into the rain and helped. Mrs. Oates leaned on her into the vestibule. Then she turned.

"Don't come up with me, Rachel. I'll be okay. Keith's here. I saw his car. You've had enough Oateses for one day." She let go of Rachel's arm. The pressure still clung there and Rachel reached out, wanting something back. But the door clicked and the woman was gone.

Heather had her pink bathrobe on. Her hair shone in the lamplight and powder smells filled the hallway. Rachel burdened her with two slightly cold but brilliant pumpkins.

"Fantastic," Heather yelled, leading her mother back into the house. Rachel saw the table set.

"I did everything I could. How's Grandma? I hope you don't have to do this every day."

"Everything's fine. Go get your drawing and I'll be right there."

At the kitchen sink Rachel turned on the water. She stood waiting for it to get warm. Though she could hear Heather's chatter in the next room and feel the light and space around her, she was still looking down, still seeing her mother-in-law's face and remembering what a doctor once told her at a cocktail party. "You wouldn't believe the number of children women are capable of having. Why even after they're dead, you can cut open the ovary and there they are—all those seeds."

Rachel bent to the water, cupping her hands. In a moment she would hold her face in the towel for as long as she needed to.

Windows

Kate is on the ladder. She's got a roll of paper towel tucked under her arm. She's permeating the film of old winter dirt with a thick spray of Windex and then wiping across and down in a definite pattern. She's slipping into something familiar, the hot sun on her arms, the jiggling of the ladder, the tops of the evergreens brushing her bare legs as she leans over to swipe at a corner. Her position on the ladder allows her an abnormal height as she looks down into her daughter's bedroom through the now clean pane.

She pauses to take in all that is there, thinking that maybe it's her position, her being able to see the room from a totally different angle that makes the looking so interesting. She's a voyeur seeing the rug running a different way, seeing the bed from the headboard down instead of the usual footboard up. And there are other things leaping into her vision.

On the bed, three books, a stack of notebook paper sliding into an arc over the side and a pile of rumpled clothing. Kate presses her face to the coolness of the glass. Brinn's underwear rolled up, piled and scrunched and then on the floor, almost kicked under her bed but not quite, a box of Kotex. Kate pulls a clean towel from the roll. She gives the top pane another squirt and works her hand in a circle. She and Brinn have talked about keeping these things rather secret, not secretive-scary, but reasonable.

Jody is only five and doesn't need to be asking a lot of questions. Brinn could learn to put her private things away. But then it is all new to her. She's had one period and Kate guesses today is the start of another, though Brinn seemed her usual crabby self, the one that can't find time to pack a school bag, dress and eat breakfast before the bus. Kate looks back into the room as if to find another explanation. There is only one. Brinn doesn't have her period again, the box simply got kicked out from under the bed.

Kate starts down the ladder, but something else moves forward in her mind, something she feels more than thinks, like a shiver to signal that she's about to topple from the ladder—Brinn does have her period, yet doesn't need to mention it to Kate—ever again.

On the ground she lifts the light aluminum ladder and moves it down the side of the house. She's almost done. She wipes her forehead and sighs, because it feels good, because that's been a response to a lot of what she's heard lately. Sighs are often pleasurable.

Her mother: *I've become a modern thinker. Well maybe not modern, but I think you do entirely too much for that man and always have. I think it's time you stop it.*

Hot sunshine on Kate's arms, the contentment of staring at a clean window, the pull of the wind at her back, the caress of air on a sweaty forehead—yes, getting things done. She backs away and looks at the house, sees so much about it that is hers—the newly painted red door, the dug out flowerbed around the tree.

Entirely too much for that man.

She wants to laugh aloud. Her mother doesn't even watch soap operas, that she knows of, but the line is so perfect.

She climbs the ladder to do one more window. She is careful holding the sides, but distracted by the bird in a bush beyond that sings a song, wee-who, wee-who, like one note up, one note down, like the squeak of an old porch swing—the bird on the swing.

"Other women have time to shop, I mean shop for parties they'll attend—or they meet for lunch or play cards. Other women—"

"God, I don't want to play cards. Spare me that."

Her mother was smoking a cigarette, the ashtray on the floor near her feet "so the smoke won't bother anyone." She'd just had her hair done, and though Kate is never really sure what that means, it looks okay, always the same. Her mother seems pleased.

"He's been out of town, right?"

"Mother, my husband's name is Ted and yes there was a business trip this week."

"Well—when is it your turn?"

Kate has trouble adjusting the ladder for this last window. The ground is uneven and the ladder wobbles and there's no one around to hold it for her. She could wait until Brinn is home, but she has to pick up Jody from Kindergarten soon and it would be great to finish.

She climbs, inching her way up. This is Jody's bedroom window, the rumpled bed inside, stuffed animals everywhere. There's never enough time.

And your children should do more. Delegate. I learned that from your father, God bless him. You don't know how to delegate. Believe me, I'd never do some of the things you do.

She balances carefully, works at each corner where

a thick layer of grime has settled. Kate on the ladder, sunshine on Kate. She's good at pushing away things her mother says. Of course she had better not fall, her mother would explode in front of Ted. And then Kate gasps, the roll of paper towel slipping out of her grasp and falling. She holds on tightly. She might be a story up. Her mother would have to nurse her, watch the children—she'd get to hear about the fall every five minutes.

She finishes by turning the soaked towel over and over until the window is clean enough. The bird is still in his swing. She starts down.

You have to say the right things to your mother, be tactful, but point things out to her. Then she'll see that you're not my slave. Ted's take on equality—they discussed what he does, what she does, and... *Think about the life your mother led when she was raising you. She didn't do her nails and shop with friends. She worked like a Trojan. I've heard some of those stories.*

Kate drops the Windex to the ground, grips the ladder and walks carefully to the shed to put it away. *She worked like a Trojan*

And the story of stories comes circling back: "When you were just a little girl, I got locked out of the house once. I was hanging the washing and the door blew shut and I was locked out. You were asleep in the upstairs bedroom and the windows were open to the breeze, so I pulled a ladder from the garage and climbed it high onto the front of the house. I prodded you with a broomstick to wake you up. I knew you were old enough to go down and open the front door for me. I was just frantic going up that ladder. I had to get back inside to you."

So how was it really, that day. She hanging laundry. Working like a Trojan. Was she panicked thinking that Kate's father would be angry for locking herself out of the house, leaving the child alone? And what was she wearing, going up the ladder—a long-skirted dress, or maybe shorts and a blouse. Or was she in high heels, her hair done, smoking a cigarette, her perfect nails clicking on the metal of the ladder. Or was there an apron, the cling of soft fabric that is warm and scented like nothing but spring air. Or a worn apron with food stains, her feet bare, the wind tossing her about, sun on her arms, drafts catching her precariously.

Was she agile, was the ladder shaking as she hurried up it? In the room—a child napping and how old, four or five, tossing in nap-sleep, drooling on the pillow. A hot day and her mother leans over to the open window and calls softly *Kate, Kate* and then prods her child gently with the end of a broom. And the edge of Kate's dream becomes a stick, becomes poking and the voice outside an upstairs window calling her name—but her mother's voice, maybe like birdsong.

Back inside the house, the phone rings.

"I'm lonely today. Could you just drop all those chores and go out to lunch with me?"

"I've got Jody. Have to get her from morning Kindergarten."

"Of course you do. She eats, doesn't she."

Kate looks out the kitchen windows. She can't hear the bird any more, can't quite remember its song as her mother's voice lingers. *I was frantic going up that ladder. I had to get back inside to you.*

Song for Her Mother

Ana couldn't remember when her desire to sing for her mother began. But it grew in her, a yearning so muscular and seductive that it blocked out her desire for anything else. For years she wouldn't sleep for all those women that came to care for her. She threw her food on the floor, clamped her mouth shut. And she filled the house with the sounds of her crying. Ana didn't even know where her mother was. She remembered wishing for death when she was only seven, not understanding why her mother abruptly walked out of their lives, and not understanding about death.

Jolene was her mother's name, and the thrill of the word upon the tongue of the abandoned child always made little Ana think of a melody, a soft wisp of music curling around her, consoling her.

Nights she lay in her bed listening for the front doorbell to chime, for footsteps across the foyer— footsteps, footsteps, her mother's footsteps. Nights her chest heaved constantly with tears that left her gasping and hiccupping so that when her physician father occasionally hugged her, she felt physical pain.

Days she stared at the various clocks in the house: a solemn grandfather in the foyer, a round brass windup that ticked and tocked in the kitchen until Ana pulled it off the counter and flung it against the wall where it bounced and slid to the floor, its life continuing—tick, tock, tick, tock. And on every day forward, until she entered high school, Ana spent time begging her father to find Jolene, bring her back. In a voice often bitter and angry, Ana's father repeatedly claimed that Jolene was sick and did not want to be found, repeatedly claimed he could do nothing. So Ana hated the Big Doc.

But she lived—first with her mother's name upon her lips, and then with the gift of music and song in her mouth, a guitar her true companion. It became a sounding board that accepted the sorrow of her feverish fingers, or gave back the thunder of her desires.

The guitar was a gift from the Big Doc. But despite this her hate for him grew in her. It reached its peak when he insisted she live with him again. Yes, he had been getting those "dead in the middle of the night" phone calls. Yes, she was just seventeen and away at school, drunk, rowdy, picked up with others by the police, not back in the dorm on time, acting strangely, seen running down the main street of the college town alone, her feet bare, toes bleeding. Yes, she had been failing all her subjects. Yes.

He told her she needed him. She needed his medical care. But she didn't want him. She feared being back, the passion of her memories swirling inside her, the house beating at her with its own set of ghosts. She clung to her guitar, telling herself that was all she needed.

At night when the beauty of the silver moonlight woke her, the pulse of creation would beat within her and Ana would reach for her guitar. Her Aunt Martha had once remarked that singing one's love meant more than just pronouncing it—singing fed the soul. Ana felt little for the woman, but these words she did not forget. She resolved to write songs that would make Jolene happy, songs that would provide both of them with an income, songs that would blow from car radios, blessing everyone on the street. Then Ana would own her own life. Jolene would hear Ana's songs and forgive her daughter's transgression, and come back. Ana had to find Jolene. She had to have her forgiveness.

Sometimes it was hard to create a song when Ana's mind was blocked with remnants of that day. She toiled with the memory, forcing it down, layering it with anger toward her father, yet sometimes bitterly asking, had it really happened that way? She told herself that she had been a stupid little kid and that was what kept Jolene away. Jolene slapped her once. Yes, that was why she left and never came back. And only that. Ana could hope.

She sifted through a melody with her fingers, responding to the voice that had followed her through the years. *Ana, Ana I'm here.* Tonight it didn't frighten her; tonight it was gentle. *Ana come to me.* So soft, not angry, sweetly close.

With her mother's name upon her tongue again, Ana began to sing:

Just to feel your eyes touching me
Just to smell your hair against my cheek,
Enchanting, your fingers lightly laced with mine
Jolene, Jolene
The stillness of us when we need not speak
The stillness of us when we need not speak

The crashing of light across the floor
The thunder of your hand across my face
Your body so opposed to mine
Jolene, Jolene
The stillness of us when we can not speak
The stillness of us when we can not speak.

But music couldn't totally heal her. And in time Ana became more desperate. She called Claire, her father's long-time secretary.

"Please, you have to find my mother. Surely he knows where she is. Please help me find her." And then as was her habit, Ana begged.

"Come stay with me for a while," Claire offered. "You know I live far out from the hospital in a small farmhouse."

"Just talk to him. Will you talk to him, please? Find out anything you can?"

"Yes, I'll try. But listen to me. You are welcome here for a while, but you'll be away from the city and all its excitement"

"I'll be away from the Big Doc," Ana said.

And they both laughed.

The first week of Ana's stay, there were endless April storms. Ana and Claire sat at a table in the candle-lit kitchen ensnared by a pattern of clattering thunder and startling, jagged light. A bowl of soup one night, a stew the next; each eaten with few words. And then one greening evening the storm blew away and Ana blurted out a rush of unstoppable words.

"The Christmas I was twelve, I went to a party at Aunt Martha's house by myself. I was terrified, fifty people talking, smoking, drinking. So much noise. But the food was incredible. Fish and pastas I'd never seen. You'd think the Big Doc's daughter ate in fancy restaurants. No, eating was a chore. But here I stuffed myself. And then it got quiet and people began to sing. One cousin played the violin. Everyone clapped and called out bravos. I had my guitar with me. It was my companion—a security blanket. I got caught up in this. I wanted to do it too. Finally I walked into the circle and said that I had a song. It was one I wrote myself. So I sang and played and they clapped and cheered. I felt the carpet tipping under me. I had to struggle to stay upright. I had never done that before, and the torment of making the decision left me exhausted."

Ana looked down at her plate, tried to calm herself. Claire was up and hugging her. Ana wanted to pretend she didn't like it—but she did.

"Ana, I'm so glad you told me."

But right then it was too much. Ana pushed away from the table and bolted out the kitchen door, ran down the sodden lawn away from Claire's touch.

The rain had stopped and Ana found a roadway that led to a dark thicket of pine trees. She needed to be in the dampness, the quiet—the shadows of the trees just filtering light. Relief filled her as she stepped onto soft beds of pine needles. She imagined if Claire or someone came after her, called out her name and she did not answer, that they would think—missing. Ana is missing.

Like her mother, her mother's child, just like Jolene.

She wondered if there wasn't a place where all missing people gathered. A place deep in a wood where the trees arched overhead to form a cathedral-like space, and underneath, a pocket of peace, a place shot through with golden light. The missing found each other there. And while they spoke and learned each other's history, more kept coming. They held out their arms to new arrivals. And they wept on each other's shoulders or picked up the children and held them and wept again. And after a time they settled into a life of waiting in stillness and quiet, until the pattern of the trees and branches against the light above them became so intense and all-consuming that their memories of those they had lost melted away. Jolene would be there with them, caught in the middle of loss, swept away on a sea of luminescence, her face upturned, her face aglow, eyes wide open, memory erased, forgiveness for her only child in her heart.

Ana broke off the newly formed twig of a fir tree. She felt the sticky pine pitch, smelled the openness of the sharp scent. Then a question, a change. Was her mother with her now? She could sense a presence, a softness, her skin prickling with the spirit of some movement and the words of Jolene's song upon her lips. She could hear the music of that song moving with the breezes that danced the branches overhead, gently moved her hair across her face. Then a hunger rose in her as if all these years the earth had never fed her.

Her mother had left her. The *Jolene* song thrummed in her head like a vicious ache

But she had abandoned her mother. She couldn't deny it any longer.

That day Jolene just appeared. Ana opened the front door and found someone standing there, all eyes in the sunlight, sunken, ringed eyes.

"Ana, my Ana." More a question than a statement. "Who are you?"

"I'm your mother. I'm Jolene."

Ana had backed away as the woman shuffled onto the foyer floor, her canvas shoes torn, revealing bulging, dirty toes. The woman wore a cotton skirt that hung longer in the front than the back, a skirt of tawdry turquoise, not a compliment to the muddy tan blouse flapping against the thin body.

"What are you doing here?" Ana couldn't take her eyes from the woman, yet at the same time she felt she was going blind. Nothing was connecting; this was not her mother.

"Hey I'm not getting a very warm welcome, though it's a scorcher out there. Could I break the ice a little here, get a hug, or a glass of cold water?"

This was not her mother. No. And in fifteen minutes the only two friends she had in the world were coming over. Six years her mother had been gone. Six years against fifteen minutes.

She turned abruptly and walked toward the kitchen. She could feel the woman following her with certainty, knowing the way. Ana took out a glass and filled it from the bottled water container. Jolene sat on one of the stools, smoothed the cloth of her skirt and settled herself at the counter. Ana's homework papers and books were scattered about.

"Ana, all these books. You're very smart, I know. Like him."

Ana swallowed, acid gripping her throat. Jolene's body gave off an odor of sadness and loneliness. Ana backed away.

"I'm okay," Jolene said. "I just had to see you. I'm still waiting for that hug."

Ana didn't move. Jolene drank water and then began to paw through Ana's papers.

"You shouldn't have come here. Why did you come here?" At first Ana didn't recognize her own voice.

"I'm better now and I had to see you. I love you, Ana. You're beautiful, you're my life."

"You left me."

"It's okay."

"It's not okay! Don't come back like this and tell me it's okay. You didn't even say goodbye. You just left me—six years ago. Do you know how long that is when you're a kid? Do you know how it feels to not have your mother?"

"I was sick. In my head. Didn't he tell you? I was afraid I would hurt you."

"You hit me once. But I needed you. I had no warning, no goodbye. I waited every day. Waited and waited. You didn't fight for me, Mama."

At first there were no words from the woman. Then, "I'm sorry. It was all I could do." The voice was flat, too controlled.

Ana reacted, the words tumbled. "I hate you. I hate you."

"You're just upset, Ana. I know you don't hate me. Or I wouldn't have come."

"It took me years to get over it. Years and years. I can't, I can't—I mean this kid I know, her dog died. And I mocked her tears. I mean a dumb dog. I lost my mother, my Mama."

"I'm sorry." Jolene robotically folded her hands in her lap.

"You aren't sorry. You're stupid and uncaring and probably drugged up and I hate you."

"Don't say that. I can be okay. We can have a friendship. I can come over in the afternoons."

The doorbell rang. A look of terror crossed over Jolene's face. A quick-change artist, in control one moment and then slipping into jelly the next. "Who is that?"

"It's him," Ana said, "the Big Doc."

"It's not him. He wouldn't ring the doorbell."

It sounded again. Ana could picture her two friends on the threshold, friends so hard to find and keep, friends so fragile.

"You can go out the back way." Ana moved toward the stool, her body a barrier, a shield to the life behind her, the life on the other side of the front door. "You have to go."

"I took my meds and then I got on the bus. It's a long way on the bus."

"I don't care. I didn't ask you to come here. I don't want you here. Do you get that?" Jolene slipped from the stood and moved toward Ana.

"Just let me hold you, Ana, just once."

"Get away from me you crazy person. Don't ever come here again and embarrass me. I don't need you anymore. God, I would never need anyone like you in my life!"

Ana can still see the devastation flooding her mother's eyes and face, still hear the stool as it tipped and crashed to the floor. But Jolene found her way, kept moving toward the back door that only the cleaning lady and the cook had ever used. Ana sensed from Jolene's movements that she held out hope that Ana would stop her, grab her in a hug. Ana did not.

Claire's search revealed that rainy April, that Jolene was dying in the county hospital where she had received care, having nowhere else to go. She'd had a stroke. In her last moments a social worker called Ana's father and he was with Jolene when she died. Ana was not. Claire drove her there a few hours later.

The nurse had combed Jolene's hair, folded her hands across her chest. Ana stood frozen in the doorway, looking around at the silent monitors, searching for her father who as always, wasn't there. She saw what looked like a meal of glasses of water, coffee and bread set out on the patient table with white linen napkins. She turned back for Claire. But she was gone too and Ana was alone. Slowly, clutching her guitar, she stepped toward the stilled body and touched the woman's cheek, staying close, drinking in the face she had not seen for years.

She had found her mother again. It was just the two of them, reunited. Ana gasped for breath and then could not see her mother's face, tears wiping away a focus, her heart leaping inside her chest as if to assail her with its life. She yearned for escape.

But she stayed. Finally taking up her guitar, she began to play.

Just to feel your eyes touching me
Just to smell your hair against my cheek,
Enchanting, your fingers lightly laced with mine
Jolene, Jolene
The stillness of us when we need not speak
The stillness of us when we need not speak

And then the voice spoke to her one last time, *Ana, my Ana. Play for me.* And Ana paused, her hands fluttering above the wood of the guitar, and then she played, singing reverently, her fingers like white darts among the strings, her words a final offering.

> *I long for you to say my name,*
> *I long for the touch of your kiss,*
> *I want your life to open to mine*
> *Jolene, Jolene*
> *The stillness of us as you leave me now,*
> *The stillness of us forever.*

Ana walked away, hurried through hallways and down staircases until once again she was out in the sunshine. She found a garden path and followed it into the hospital grounds where magnolia trees lined it, their petals thick and fragrant, petals now littering and spangling the greening lawn with white, spilling onto the pebbly stone so that Ana crushed them with her walking. A gust of wind swept through the branches, cascading more petals down on Ana, sifting them onto her shoulders, catching them in the strands of her hair. Shreds of perfume from the trees surrounded her and she bent to the ground and picked up petals, lifted them to her mouth to taste the perfume. She thought of the bread someone had set out on Jolene's table—food for those who mourn, release from hunger.

You Have Done Nothing Wrong

"Sunny. Are you in here? Sunny!"

Elise Mathews in a flaring skirt and her coat-length sweater paced the cement floor at the front of the greenhouse. Her leather bag bumped on her stomach.

"Sun-ny!"

Wind rattled the greenhouse windows; sheets of plastic that covered some of the cultivars snapped and flicked in the air rushing through the vented ceiling. Known to follow her instincts, Elise Mathews had forced herself out of bed this dark morning to phone Sunny about the predicted weather and how that would affect her upcoming garden project. Though she had no plans for the day, Elise was annoyed that Sunny wasn't right there in the greenhouse waiting for her. Sunny had promised. What was the matter with the woman? Even her desk was tidy, no plans for Elise's project out and waiting. As agitation built in Elise, she rooted around in her voluminous bag for her cell phone. She'd call Sunny, who obviously was still in the house—get her over here.

And then for a moment the space was still, the sky holding its breath, waiting to send the first light flicks of rain down against the greenhouse windows. And Elise heard something fall—something light that bounced and rolled. At the back. At the back of the greenhouse in the stuffy lean-to where she and Sunny always joked about having tea.

"Sunny?" Elise moved slowly down one of the greenhouse aisles trying not to knock over plants and seedpods with her purse or generous frame. The wind had blown open the door to the lean-to. There Elise's foot kicked a prescription bottle causing it to roll back into the room to rest by Colette, Sunny's college-age daughter, who lay sprawled on the floor.

Elise thought Sunny would scream, that her cries might rise above the thunder din, the blaze in her eyes reflect eerie flashes of light that now slashed through the space changing it into a truly *sickening-green* house.

Being a social worker, Elise had actually seen mothers tear out their hair when faced with children's death attempts; one woman picked up the bloody blade and tried to use it on her own wrist.

Colette's was a quiet attempt, a soundless swallowing of many pills.

Sunny tore into the room, dropping on her knees to her daughter. Elise had first called 911 and given the street address. After reaching Sunny in the house, she called 911 again because Sunny was stammering and shouting about directions, about speed, that the ambulance could get to Colette and the hospital faster if they used the greenhouse delivery entrance.

Sunny's hair was matted to her head, wet from the shower. Elise was familiar with the transformation. You could dismiss restraint and correctness in the grip of death; you could count on anger and fear splitting and slicing through the skin of calm; you could count on torment—shouting this:

"It's me, Colette. I'm here. Your mother is here. You will be okay. I'm not mad at you. You will be okay. I love you. I'm not mad at you it will be okay. My God, Colette, it will be okay. You have done nothing wrong. Nothing."

Then for Sunny, another change, moments of composure, allowing her to feel a pulse in the daughter's neck, make sure that Elise had turned Colette's head to the side in case the girl vomited, and finally causing her trembling voice to become softer as it continued the mantra: *It's me, Colette, it's your Mom.*

As she stood there, Elise remembered the woman she'd heard much about but never met, Sunny's mother Marilyn, who was visiting this Labor Day weekend, who could increase the burden of daughter and granddaughter with her very presence. And right then, Marilyn appeared.

Elise felt the horrendous, twisted desire to laugh in a bleak situation—to want the black humor that pushed reality away making you forget death—death that clung and pulled at you, paring away protective layers, leaving you open to raw and frightening life. For Marilyn wore red pants and a pink shirt, tawny lipstick. Her graying hair was askew and wiry, an electric current of emotion spinning around her head. She stood off to the side and Elise knew what that was about. You are trying to believe what you see; you are trying to make it real—your granddaughter lying barely breathing on the floor with her mother's lovely plants all around and the shock of a storm pounding overhead.

Later, while a team was working on Colette, Sunny wasn't really alone, just off in a corner of the hospital visiting area, her arms locked across her chest as she tried to get hold of herself, fought to not notice the couple in the corner, heads together, silently crying, or the tense older man who sat in a wheel chair coughing into a series of paper napkins which he then dropped to the floor.

There were things she would not allow herself to think about. And there were things that she would:

—the spindle chair at her desk in the greenhouse; in its life, before it was hers, the chair was a vivid turquoise; now only strips and scratches on the seat revealed such a color, like water coming up through the wood; she found the chair, tipped over in overgrown grass by a shed at one of her suppliers; she asked to pay for it, but the guy, Charlie, said *just take the old thing*;

—the plank table, just beyond the desk and chair, that her husband, Hunter, had made for her using leftover lumber from the greenhouse construction; they had slapped glossy white paint on it and hung four utility lights above, securing the electric supply to the slanted rafters; under the lights she could picture her pots of fuzzy lamb's ear, trailing sweet potato vine, and eucalyptus; she could almost smell the eucalyptus;

—and the long ceramic horse trough that she used for a sink; Hunter had found it, she didn't know where, lugged it home in the back of his truck; it was noon and she remembered a swelling of something much more than happiness, closer to pure joy as he pulled into the driveway, then lifted the trough covered with a blanket with his strong arms, presenting to her the prize that finished her greenhouse; Hunter…

—and the couple, a lithe girl and a skinny overly tall boy, kissing in front of the post office; open to the world, big and joyful in their lips together, their hips meeting, yet so small in the context of life; how big the oak trees were above them, how thick the cement blocks of the post office; yet their fingers joining were hollow thin bones, easy to crack; such realizations could deaden Sunny's desire, her search for some elation and a miracle of change; but did it really matter if it did; those two kids, anyone, everyone—floated out there on their own, thinking they were going to make change; big muscular change; she and Hunter now shrinking in their space, with sorrows maybe insignificant in the face of a paralyzing car accident, a sudden death, a suicide attempt; yes theirs owned infidelity, betrayal; and they'd had their turn, their muscles now atrophied, the big and joyful over;

—but not the girls; please not Colette and Jessica—their lives were just starting. Both of them.

Sunny sat by the bed, watching Colette's astonishing hair spread out over the pillow. The profundity of it. From glossy filaments and tendrils in her baby pictures had burst this mass. It was like recognizing power in an infinitesimal seed, a coil of energy ready to spring, Colette's hair pouring from her scalp in autumnal brightness. But what else was Colette germinating? What other thoughts lurked in the cortex of her brain that would suddenly unfurl into such madness? She didn't have to take pills. Didn't she know that?

Sunny clutched a handful of bed sheet. She held on. There was too much beauty in the leaping grass beyond her greenhouse—oh why hadn't Colette just looked out before she thought of pills—too much beauty in the hair spread along the white pillow—there would be no squandering of this life. Whatever pain Colette had, she could talk to her mother about it. Now Sunny would make sure.

The girl moved and turned, opened her eyes.

Sunny offered a few sips of water. After a while: "Colette, you didn't want to die, did you?"

"I don't know, won't go there."

"I love you. Here, hold my hand."

After a while: "I couldn't tell you things. I told Dad. I wanted to hurt him. Really hurt him. I hate the way he treats you."

"That's just between the two of us, Colette."

"Don't do that. Defend him like that. He needs to make it right by you, whatever he's done."

"What did you tell him that you haven't told me? Was it like in high school?"

"I can't do this."

"Okay. But—"

"I get so confused. There was this guy and then he dropped me and so I started flirting at the coffee house and then these other girls asked me to stay over. They were making money—yeah like high school. I was in control. No one could hurt me."

"Except yourself. We talked about this when it happened before. The guy likes it. You are demeaning yourself."

"I like it. I like feeling that I can control them, the erection, the whole thing."

Sunny was overtaken. But she couldn't bury herself anymore, even though it would feel so relieving and cleansing if she could go somewhere and explode. But she would stay, because Colette might say something to blot out or hopefully alter the present conversation. So Sunny looked into the pasty face of her daughter, knowing it was worth the effort to put it out there another way.

"You are never in control of another human being, Colette. Especially a man, especially the man you might think you love. Each is in his own control. You are demeaning yourself. Engage them with your eyes, with the tilt of your head. You don't have to give away something so intimate. You risk disease. But more you risk losing yourself. You know that."

"Maybe."

"Colette, I gave you information, but I tried to raise you so that you would understand the power of your body and the beauty of having children and how great intimacy with a man can be. I mean, how did I go wrong? I had none of what you had. I learned about sex reading my father's books, piecing the information together. That was it."

The nurse poked her head in, "If you don't mind, Mrs. Garland, I'd like to help Colette up to the bathroom."

"I can—"

"We worry about falls. I'll take her this time. You might want to get a cup of coffee?"

Sunny nodded. The old coffee trick to get *mommy* out of the room so the nurse could get the true assessment of how Colette was feeling just hours after trying to kill herself.

Sunny sat with the coffee, remembering her confusion when overnight Colette seemed to be sexually active and Sunny ill-equipped to deal with the situation. So much so that she had questioned the development of her own sexuality, wondering if it was part of Colette's angst and Hunter's cheating, though neither of them knew her secrets.

Sunny, lured into a sexual relationship by Professor Burnquist when she was only nineteen and he in his forties, had abruptly ended it, and from then on completely denied any sexual yearning in order to live with the sordid history. For years. Before Hunter. What a mistake, because the yearning was truly good and natural, something she should have allowed to happen.

It took years for her to reason and see that her body had a place on the planet in all its physical roundness and beauty, as important a body as those of African women in the National Geographic pictures her mother thrust in front of her. As they faced the camera, smiling women with full breasts, sure of themselves, happy and never ashamed—her mother poked at the page saying they were like naughty children. Sunny waved the words away.

It's a cultural thing, Marilyn. Stay out of my head and let me be free from the tentacles of bad decisions; and if I'm still not in balance, I will work hard to find one. That's the upside; that's the good news.

Then came the worries that her ambivalence about her sexual past would somehow scar her daughters. She hated to even think about it, remembering when she had stumbled upon Colette's talk with a friend and Sunny had not been able to let it go.

"Colette. I heard what you said to Julia." This blurted out after she made an excuse to lure the teenager, get her into the car and drive to the mall—didn't Colette need a new pair of jeans? "I heard you telling Julia that you gave more than one of those boys good head. At her party. Tell me that's not true."

"You had no right to listen."

"I am your mother." Each word strung out. She tried to calm herself. "I care about the things you do."

"It's my business."

"It's scary business." Sunny clenched the steering wheel.

"Don't exaggerate or anything, Mom. Cause you

look like you might explode or something. I mean. Don't blow it out of proportion."

"I, I can hardly say the words."

"That's your problem. You're afraid of this stuff but—oh shit, I'm not going there. Your problem."

"If you stop doing this I won't tell your father." Where did that come from?

"What? What does that mean. What's he going to do—ground me? It's my life."

"Colette please. I want you to be happy. Normal happy. You're my child, my daughter. I mean we have to talk about these things. So you were experimenting. So now it's over. Right? You'll think of your reputation and the diseases you could get. You'll—"

And that's when Sunny slammed into the car in front of her starting a series of fender benders. Colette got a sore neck, Sunny's more serious, a whiplash that required a collar. Hunter appeared at the hospital to help deal with the car and the insurance. No jeans were purchased. She remembered she made up a few more sentences in her head to share with Colette, but ended up not saying anything else about the subject, hoping that Colette would heed her warnings. And it was a time when Hunter was often off picketing abortion clinics and every time she saw him, she just could not engage him in the subject. Then she read some of his picketing signs in the back of his truck and in a fury, dropped the idea completely.

After Colette came home, dinners began again, mostly flung together at the last minute, Marilyn setting the table, Sunny frying fish and tossing a salad, and occasionally Hunter coming home in time to grill hamburgers.

It wasn't the Brady bunch. It wasn't sweet lemonade with flowers on the table and saucy chatter right through to dessert. There were lots of pauses and silences when cutlery hit the plates and people chewed.

Sunny worried that Marilyn would try to alter the natural course of things and talk about the foibles of rock stars or the danger of melting glaciers or bore them with the lives of the people she played bingo with. But she did not. And she had never said anything that a woman her age might say revealing an inability to understand what had happened to her granddaughter. The exact opposite.

Not only did Marilyn offer encouragement to the younger daughter, Jessica, no matter what the subject—an unfair grade or a nasty comment from someone at school about Colette—but also on those nights when Colette did come to the table, Marilyn seemed to breathe in her every movement, holding people around her granddaughter at bay with her eyes. If Sunny was about to leap on something Colette had said, she would feel Marilyn's gaze upon her. Sunny wasn't sure why this was happening. It was almost as if Marilyn had become Elise at the table, Elise with her years of social work and her sensitivity to social issues. Marilyn got Colette's pain and would defend her from any insinuations. Colette was seeing a counselor. Colette was not going back to school this semester. She had overdosed on pills. She had to work through her problems. For now, with everything else attacking the peaceful fabric of their family life, that was that—until Sunny and Hunter came to grips with the rips in their marriage.

Making Change

"Hon, do you have any change?" My husband was calling to me.

"I'm not sure. Wait a moment." I was brushing my hair, looking for wrinkles in the mirror and brushing. It was raining outside and in the grey light my face was ashen.

"Hurry Emily," he called again. "I have to take the toll road today."

"Okay," I said coming out of the bathroom. I opened a kitchen drawer, handed him nickels and quarters.

"Your hands are so cold."

"It's chilly this morning," I said into his shoulder as he held me. I loved feeling the soft texture of his suit, the warmth of his body. But he was already away from me, his mind racing, his schedule beating inside his head. He let go of me and grabbed his raincoat.

"Now call me," he said. "When is your doctor's appointment? I'm worried about you."

"One o'clock. I'll call you."

"And don't forget to put those suits out for the Goodwill please. I want to make room for some new stuff I'm going to buy."

"Will do."

He reached out, touching my hair with one hand

and jangling change in his pocket with the other.

"Your plane leaves at six tonight, Kent, but you didn't tell me what hotel you'll be staying in."

"I've got a three o'clock meeting. I'll let you know when we talk. I forget those little details. But the facts and figures—those are on my lips." He smiled, kissed me lightly. "Going to land this one, Em."

"I'll miss you."

"It's just a night."

"I never sleep well. The walls of the house seem to expand…"

"I hate hotel rooms." He kissed me again.

Through a wet window I watched him drive away. And then the phone was ringing.

"Hello," I said in my grey voice.

"Emily!" The voice was breathy, excited.

"Veda?" I said hesitating.

"Of course. Did you forget that I was in town to-day?" Knowing Veda would not wait for me to answer, but would go on to tell me about her latest cruise, or the crepes she had for breakfast, I hastily scanned my calendar and found the scrawled note: Veda, three o'clock.

"My mind, I completely forgot. But I'll make it. But I might be late…"

I stopped. She had interrupted, asking me what I would like her to order from room service.

"Veda, don't fuss. You see…"

"But Em, it's been six months or more. We have to celebrate our reunion. Now if you're going to be late, we'll have tea together. I know they can send us a real English tea."

"Veda, a lot has happened since we talked."

"Oh, what?" Veda's voice was a whisper. I tried to think of my next line, my cue, but all I could do was look out my kitchen window and watch brown leaves falling with the rain.

"Well?" The breathless voice. It silenced me so that I could listen. As I stared at Kent's uneaten toast, I could hear the voice ordering lobster, white wine, or exclaiming over the scent of roses. Veda had married a wealthy older man, had no children, and travelled. We'd seen each other only a handful of times since college. But that voice always drew me in.

"We'll talk when I get there," I finally said. "What's your suite number?" I wrote it down. I had been right saying *suite* not *room* and I didn't need to ask the hotel as Veda always stayed at the Drake when she was in Chicago.

The called ended, her voice lingering until the whistling teakettle erased it. I turned it off, holding my hands over the steaming spout to let the vapors warm them. But soon I had no choice, I had to move, make tea, plan what I would wear on a wet cold November day that included a dreaded doctor's appointment and now a visit with Veda.

The house swelled with silence as I climbed the stairs, stopping on the landing to look out at the sweep of roof and the yard below. Birds fluttered in the gutters like heavy leaves, their heads bent, their beaks pushing aside twigs and decay looking for food in rhythmic, instinctive movements. They knew what they needed, and they knew where to search for it.

Opening my closet door, I stood for a long time just staring, not knowing what to wear. Finally I reached for an old standby, a thick brown wool suit that though I tried, I couldn't seem to part with. I drank my hot tea as I dressed. The spattering of rain on the window and even the ticking of Kent's small brass clock filled the room with a jagged union of sounds that seemed to beat *why me?* If only I could fly away on a plane, or lose myself on some cruise or just find something amazing! I had even tried reading the want ads—but there was no clue there.

Walking the still hallway, I peered into Nicholas's room, then Terry's. Autumn and college had made great changes, the strong winds of packing sweeping away the posters, the guitars, the music collections. Each was now neat and barren. "You don't have to hold down the fort any more," Kent said as we drove from Terry's campus. "You're free to do anything." For a week we had gone out to dinner. He bought me flowers. But then the traveling began again and the phone rang. "Mother," Terry said, "I desperately need more pants." "Hi Mom, it's Nick. I hate to ask you this, but could you run out and buy me a leather jacket? And it has to be dark brown." The fort was empty; there were no replacements, and yet no true relief in sight.

My doctor was in the city. I accelerated and braked along the traffic-laden expressway envisioning scarlet leaves and a stretch of green lawn lit by late, angular fall sunlight. But the image faded as I finally turned off, automatically switching lanes for the three-mile drive to the Medical Center. This autumn I had never found the time to see the image; Veda surely could share it with me. She'd probably fit in a trip to the New England hills between a cruise to Prague and then Hawaii. She was always going somewhere. My time had been spent focusing inward, using my sense of *something is just not right*, more than sight or touch. I had to discover what was *off* with me.

"This is common in women your age," my gynecologist said. "You'll be much happier after the surgery. Try not to worry; in most cases the tumors are benign."

I parked the car, rode the elevator to the main level, and then sat in a waiting room until a nurse handed me lab papers and directions. Then I was directed to another waiting room. Endless. Finally at two-thirty, they were doing some tests, pulling blood from my arm, my blood—as rich a red as any autumn leaf. The technician filled five little tubes, set them on a counter next to a brilliant pumpkin and directed me back to the first waiting room.

The Medical Center was hyper with people, some in wheelchairs, some on crutches, others begin rolled back and forth on gurneys by attendants in bright green scrubs. I watched them going in and out of an elevator that I knew could suck me up into the center of the building and hide me away in some surgical suite. I thought about how warm the dishwater would feel if I were home cleaning up. I imagined the invigorating whip of wet wind that would surround me as I raked leaves in the rain. But I sat.

For a while I tired to trick my mind, pretend I was younger and pregnant, waiting for a checkup. But the game was just that. Going to the doctor's had meant reading maternity magazines in the waiting area and then getting the news in a pink or blue examining room that my weight was good and the baby was developing nicely. Now the magazines I picked up advised about sunscreen to prevent skin cancers, diets and exercise to ward off weight gain and its companion, diabetes. Some doctors mumbled, didn't smile, didn't look at me when delivering news. But surely my gynecologist had the right to look directly at me; after all, none of this was his fault.

"Mrs. Willard."

As I sat half-dressed by the doctor's desk, I noticed the nurse had left my chart. Opening it, I read my name, my address, but then the rest of the words blurred; they seemed to refer to some other person. I put the chart back, better to just sit and wait.

"Mrs. Willard, how are you?" The doctor hurried into the room and took up my chart. "Well..." he was reading. Then, "The results of all your tests conclude that you'll definitely be having surgery. But we suspected this all along. A fibroid tumor like yours often gives a women trouble during menopause. But the pain, the excessive periods will soon be ancient history."

"I feel like ancient history," I said. At the moment I didn't like this man, even though he had delivered my children. I noticed his sideburns had turned silver. "And you'll do the surgery?"

"Yes. You're scheduled for a week from Thursday. My nurse will call you tomorrow with some preliminary instructions. Do you have any questions now?"

"No. I just don't like waiting."

"You'll be fine. Don't worry and enjoy the rest of your day."

I walked out, walked past some women who were truly waiting, their abdomen's swelling with life, their faces looking off into some secret space of layettes and nursery decorating. I wasn't one of them. But did I even want to be? I was walking around with an organ, a once miracle-working organism, now a uterus that had to come out. A week from Thursday.

The floors of the Medical Center were newly washed. Little metal signs informed me to walk with care. But even though I already was, I got lost. I had to ask someone to direct me to the main entrance. When I called Kent's office, I got his voice recording. I checked my watch—2:55 p.m. So prompt Kent, for a 3:00 o'clock meeting. I left a brief message.

Driving, I played my fantasy game. I was a singer today, on my way to meet my agent and dine on truffles, whatever they were. Other days I had been an interior designer and I had even run away and married another man, a stranger who didn't like to travel.

Fantasies were appropriate today as Veda's life was like a fantasy. In the past it had been a lark to leave the kids with a sitter and sit in her hotel room whose elegance was defined by heavy draperies and heavier furniture. I would listen to details of her trips, her decorating, her wardrobe, then drive home, dreaming of something like that for me. But in the driveway life always rushed in on me again—Terry hugging me, pulling me from the car, Nicholas demonstrating a jump shot or some perilous new bike trick.

Today. What would I talk about with Veda?

I drove the tunnel-like lanes of the parking garage picturing my rain-soaked driveway and my darkened house. I wanted to be there.

"Emily!" Veda bear-hugged me in the doorway of the suite. "What kept you?"

I took off my damp raincoat and folded it over my arm. Veda was already deep into the room, pouring me a cup of tea and talking about the view from her window. I walked over to see, hearing about it as she talked, seeing it through her eyes more than my own. Veda saw a choppy lake. "Those waves are so exciting to watch! See that tiny boat adrift, all alone? No, Em, that way." I watched her long fingers pointing and marking off the landmarks of her view. Then she handed me a cup of tea and I sank down into the cushions, still holding my damp coat. It was always like that with Veda.

"Why are you late? I was waiting."

"I had to see my gynecologist. At the Medical Center. And of course everyone was running late."

"Go on."

"I have to have a hysterectomy."

"I see. When? Right away?" Veda asked looking down to brush cookie flakes from the skirt of her plum-colored dress.

"A week from Thursday. I have a tumor. Fibroid. They're usually benign."

"They're always benign," Veda said.

"That's my news."

"You'll be fine." Her breathless voice was soft, soothing. "Millions of women have that happen to them, millions."

I picked up a teacake.

"Anyway, you can loll around, let Kent take care of things. He's so efficient. Sounds good to me."

"Maybe," I said wondering.

"You'll be a trooper. Like you always are."

"Kent travels a lot," I said, noticing the silver rings that laced both of Veda's hands. "I mean this is inconvenient. Bad timing on my part. Anyway, how are you and Chuck? Is he here?"

"I just finished a cruise. South America. He's back home, working." Suddenly her voice sounded like mine, flat and tired. We sat for a while drinking tea, trying different choices from the tray.

The hotel phone rang. Veda smiled and jumped up, walking over to an elegant desk to answer it. I imagined her in her own home. She'd shown me photos, so

I knew her life.

"How nice to talk to you. Yes, it's been a very long time. Certainly. She's right here."

Veda was extending the phone to me. "It's Kent."

I glanced at my watch, picturing him at the airport. It was just past four. "Kent, hi, where are you?"

"I got your message. Easy to track you down cause it's always the Drake."

"Yes, it always is."

"What's the report?"

"A week from Thursday."

"What?"

"The surgery is a week from Thursday."

"Oh, Hon, is that soon enough?"

"Yes. No hurry, no worry."

"I'll put it on my calendar."

"I love you, Kent."

"Me too. I don't have much time. Sorry. Change in plans."

"What change?"

"McDonald. He's meeting me in Minneapolis and he has tickets for the Guthrie tomorrow night."

"But I thought you were coming home mid-morning."

"Why don't I get you a ticket and you can fly out tomorrow and meet us."

"But it's a business thing."

"Not really. He's just thanking me for some work. Say *yes*. Spur of the moment's the best."

I looked down at my brown wool suit. The hem of the skirt was damp and limp like the brown leaves piling in the side yard. Then I looked over at Veda. She had left the tea and was standing alone at the window.

"I can't go, Kent."

"Why not?" The question had an edge.

"I'm having surgery. And—"

"You'll be fine, Emily."

"I don't feel fine. I feel, well, confused. I need time to think."

She could feel him pausing, preparing his words carefully.

"Okay. I understand."

"I've, I've got things to do. Before." Veda had come away from the window. She was frowning at me.

"You just sounded so wistful this morning. So when this came up, I thought that maybe. And I know McDonald would enjoy seeing you."

"McDonald can see me another time." Silence. Then—"I just want to go home, Kent. Okay? It doesn't go away with words. And then after, there's recuperation. I'll need you. I'll need the kids. I mean I'll have to rely on all of you a lot."

"We'll be there. You know we will."

"For a while you'll have to do things you're not used to doing."

"Of course. We'll work everything out. Are you okay now, Emily?"

"Truthfully, no. I feel lousy."

"I can cancel this trip."

"No. I want you to go."

"I'll call you as soon as I land."

"That's fine."

"I love you, Emily." The words were strong, strong enough to allow the call to end.

"Veda," I said, moving toward the plump sofa, "how about more of that tea." Veda poured, then sat opposite me, twisting her amethyst ring. "Maybe you should have gone. Flown there tomorrow."

"If he asked me for a quiet weekend, fine. Would you have gone, with Chuck?"

"It's confusing. I always tagged along when he wanted me to, but it's never been enough."

"Enough. What do you mean?"

"We don't see eye to eye on things. We spend most of our time, well, separated."

"Veda."

"It's okay. It's been like that for a long time. You knew."

I heard the voice. I watched the long fingers selecting another teacake. Then I looked at her intently. The plum-colored dress was too garish, making her skin look sallow, like mine. And her hair, crumpled and frizzy from too many perms and dye experiments, echoed the present condition of my hair that truly needed a good styling.

"We're a pair," I finally said. "You marry to spend a lifetime with a man and you hardly ever see him. You picture your life as you'd like it to be and it never works out. It's crazy."

"But Emily, you life has worked out. You have everything. You married the best looking and the smartest guy in our group and he's still in love with you. And you are still in love with him. And you have two successful children."

I stared at her. "I always envied you, Veda, always." I looked away, reaching for my purse, knocking it to the floor.

"Em, are you okay? Did I—"

"I'll be fine," I said, lowering myself to the floor, moving on my knees to retrieve a rolling lipstick and my purse. A squashed tissue gave me comfort as I walked over to the window to stare at the lake, dab at my eyes.

Finally I said, "Veda, have you ever eaten truffles?"

"Yes, in my opinion, they're awful."

I began to laugh, tears still welling in my eyes. "Somehow I knew you'd say that."

"It's true. Now come over here and sit down."

I walked slowly, taking a teacake as I passed by the tray.

"I'm being blunt today," Veda said, "but we're big girls now." She hesitated. "You know I've been angry at you for something for a long time, Em."

I stared at her, this woman of plum and silver, stared at her as if she were a stranger.

"Do you know what it is?"

"No, Veda, I don't know."

"Senior year, you told Sharon, my roommate, and she told me. You said Veda commands attention but she doesn't earn it."

Her words deprived me of gravity. I was falling, falling into the past and finding nothing to grab on to. I watched Veda tilt her head. Maybe she was looking at my damp brown suit or my grey face. I heard myself say, "That was a compliment. A compliment. What I meant was, you didn't have to earn it; it was yours for the taking."

"I don't think that's what you meant," Veda said.

Anger rose in me as we faced each other across a tea table, across years of her hurried visits that amounted to little true maintenance of our friendship.

"Aren't you quibbling?" I asked, stifling my anger. "Is it really important to you, one thing I said and after all these years?"

"Of course. I've always felt that what you say is important. You have to know that. You're my closest friend, Em. All these years I was just afraid to bring it up."

I was stunned into silence.

"Do you command or earn attention, Emily?"

"Me?" I laughed. "It's a different kind of attention and I've really worked myself into it. Sometimes I feel like I'm indispensable. Well, almost. To my family."

"Are you complaining?" There was a catch in Veda's voice.

"To be very honest, yes. I need to get going again, and I need to go in one direction. After all, there's suddenly not enough of me to go around."

"What direction do you want to go in?"

"Oh Veda, all these questions. Let's talk about your cruise or something."

"I really just want to hear your good ideas. You always have good ideas."

I really saw her now, sitting there across from me, she with the same wrinkles that I had, the same touch of grey in her hair, the same question on her face. The very same question. As I spoke, I wondered if she too hesitated in front of her closet each morning. "I don't know if I have any good ideas, Veda. I'm searching and I guess I'll land on my feet. You will too."

She was quiet, studying her rings.

"Veda. Well, look—you haven't been to my home in twenty years or more. Please come home with me tonight. Stay a few days. We'll have lots of time to talk. We'll figure everything out. The two of us."

"I'd like that, Em, but I can't." Her eyes pleaded with me to understand. Possibly we had come far enough in one hour.

"That's okay. You'll be back soon. Please plan on staying with me next time."

"And you'll be feeling well and everything. I mean even with the surgery." Now the voice rang like a bell as she watched me rise and reach for my purse.

"I'll be fine. But I really must go. It's been good talking like this." I threw my raincoat over my arm and we walked to the door. This time when we hugged, it felt like Veda wanted to hang on to me for a very long time.

A fine mist of rain still fell. I drove home, my head filling with concrete plans. I could always read the want ads during my recuperation. There were books on planning your future with lots of great ideas for "cottage industry" work. And I had a friend who knew everything there was to know about volunteer work. The perks of the surgery? My family would finally fly by themselves. And I would be fine. I would have my own life. Funny, a day with Veda had always led to fantasy, but today it drove me down the real road.

As I pulled into my driveway an hour later, warm light glowed in the living room windows. Kent had remembered to fix the light timer.

I let myself in and climbed the stairs. Opening my closet, I searched for my comforting terry cloth robe— not there. Surely it was in Kent's closet as our robes are the same color—and yet there were his suits for Goodwill, pushed to one side and properly labeled *GOODWILL* in black marker on a sheet of paper. I pulled them out and tossed them on the bed, just as the phone rang.

"Kent," I said.

"You okay, Emily? You sound out of breath."

"I'm fine. Just doing a few things."

We talked. We shared words of love for one another—easily and openly. When we hung up, I found my mind singing *Why me Why me*—an invigorating question, not a complaining one. Why me to be so lucky to have all that I did have? Why me to now be eager for the future, no matter what it brought?

At last I took off my damp brown suit. With a smile and a *heave ho* I flung it onto the Goodwill pile. I didn't even hesitate.

P.S. Reader, this story was written before laparoscopic surgery, thus the recuperation period could be quite lengthy.

Hazel's Child

Hazel Enright sat on one of the sun-warmed benches on the church patio. She turned her face upwards to catch some rays, the usual bright red flower she wore tucked just behind her right ear, a startling contrast to her grey hair. She was meeting Hunter Garland to discuss changes in the church programs he ran for teens and women. The head of United In Jesus Church, Reverend Porter, had insisted that Hazel discuss any ideas she had with Hunter.

"You two can work together," Porter told her. "Your background counseling women in hospitals should convince Hunter how perfect you are for his prolife work."

That day Hazel had merely smiled and walked away, Porter distracted by church members eager to shake his hand, congratulate him on his sermon. Hunter Garland believed in picketing the Heartworld Clinic. That made Hazel crazy.

A shadow blocked her sunlight.

"Hazel, hello."

She watched him fight for something in his suit coat pocket, finally pulling out a cell phone that he quickly shut off.

"There. Well, it's good to meet with you." And Hunter Garland sat on the bench opposite her. She noticed that his voice was grainy, like he hadn't used it for a while.

"I know you don't mean that, Hunter. It's kind of you to pretend that you want to work with me, but I know there's no love lost between us."

"Well, I think Reverend Porter wants us, or me, to get beyond that. At this point, I'm willing."

Hazel felt Hunter's nervousness as he tried to hold her in his vision. She reached up and touched the red flower.

"It might be good for you to just come right out and tell me what it is about me that irritates you. My age? The way I dress?"

"There's nothing—I mean why would you say that?"

"You like to work with younger women. I'm seventy years old. And I break the dress code for old people with my jeans and my clogs."

"Reverend tells me you're a nurse."

"Certainly not!" Hazel's words were crisp, bordering on angry.

"But you do hospital work?"

"I do."

Hunter leaned forward, resting his elbows on his knees. "Hazel, could you please tell me about that."

"I've worked in hospitals forever. I was the oldest candy striper on record in Detroit. From there I worked in the hospital gift shop, the cafeteria, then graduated to helping log in sterile packs in the sterile prep department. After a while I agreed to work in admissions. I just needed to be there."

"Why?"

"I wanted to find and help women—single married young older, who had miscarried or lost a child through stillbirth or death right after birth. Or in some cases abortion. "

"And your reason?"

"So I could sit with them."

"Sit with them?"

"I found these women. Got their room numbers. After my duties were completed, I would wait, until they were alone. Then I would enter and introduce myself as a silent counselor. I would close the door to the noises of the hallway and just sit with them in that stillness, holding a hand or hugging them. They all confessed that they couldn't bear to hear words. Especially the words doctors and nurses often say: you'll have another baby; you're young; this is nature's way; this is God's will; it was just meant to be. Or some parent might say to a teen: you're better off. You could burn in hell. Whatever."

"I see," Hunter said, the words, slow, hesitant.

"Do you."

"But your methods were not, well, honest."

"No. I was honest."

"But not official. Do I mean trained?" He rubbed his forehead as if to erase a thought or bring to light another thought.

"Many men steer clear of these things, Hunter Garland. I am certain there is something in your life that also draws you to prolife and these issues."

"What were you referring to with the 'no love lost between us' comment?" Hunter asked. She could almost feel his eyes on her red flower.

"You don't hear what you don't want to hear. I've attended five of your meetings. I've talked against some of your tactics. And very openly. You know that. I abhor the picketing in front of clinics. I'll not mince words. I would do anything to stop that."

"But we are prolife—"

"I sit with women in hospital rooms. I know what's going on in their heads. I know they are scared and sick at heart and that having to cross a picket line of people with signs will not move them toward a different decision."

"How do you know any of this?" His voice trembled between a formed question and a shout of anger.

"I know that these women eventually want to talk. And I want them to be able to tell their stories, to me, to you—after the stillness, after they have lived for a while with the experience. I want them to use their voices."

He said nothing, moving his sleeve up to check his watch.

"We have to make time to help people, Hunter Garland."

"Then why work with me? I don't see the connection. It's too late for these women you talk to, the ones that have already had an abortion. Too late. The damage is done. You are obviously not a rule follower, so this meeting is pointless. Maybe you could sign up to bring brownies to our meetings."

"I'll ignore that last comment. I know you don't mean what you say about damage. It's not just preventing abortion we should be concerned about, but the circumstances of the pregnancy, the mindset of the girl or woman, the support she is or isn't getting, how she is before she's pregnant, how she will be after—her mental state, you might say. Her understanding. And of course whether she has an abortion or not. This is how we will change things. It's a big picture. You are only looking at one small part of it."

"It's the only part that counts, Hazel. We stop clinics and doctors. We change the laws. That's our goal. The rest will follow."

"And after you have achieved all of this your daughter Jessica comes to you or your wife and thinks she is pregnant. How old is your daughter right now?"

"You have absolutely no right to bring my daughter into this." And he stood up, looking around just as the back door to the church opened and Reverend Porter's secretary, Connie, leaned out.

"Mr. Garland. Your cell phone must be off. There's a call for you. Someone is trying to find you."

He moved toward the door, flapping a hand over his shoulder to let Hazel know he would be back.

She turned away, raising her face again to the warmth of the sunlight; she smiled to herself. This Hunter Garland would be tougher than she thought. But she had ways to get to him. She had to get to him. There had to be major changes in all his committees and the way he used church funds. And what if the fates were kind and he resigned under her pressure?

Every piece of armor had a chink. Hunter might have more than one—something he had once felt or lived. Because something had led him to his ministry and the fierce grip he had to have on it.

Hazel had her own memories to push her forward. And when she was angry, like right now, they came back bold, clear and painful.

Odd things would bring the time to mind: hard-boiled eggs—she was less than polite when anyone served them to her. She could still feel them clutching at her throat, the dryness of the yolk spreading out to choke her, the reprimand that food wasn't cheap and she should eat everything on her plate. The smack on the back of her head, occasionally, a crowning symbol of the moment. So thank you, Miss Davis.

Or a thick woods, deep and dark with conifers. That would make her tremble. The home had stood in a clearing surrounded by pine trees. She had vomited out the window of the black sedan when her father's driver pulled off the narrow tarred road that twisted through the woods, crunching on a gravel drive. At first she told herself that the fearful dark forest could be a source of comfort during those months. It would protect her from outside sorrows. She could stare at it from her window and get lost in her thoughts. But her window was set back, part of an older wing of the building, so that she looked down on more of the circular gravel driveway where delivery trucks turned in and emptied their contents: cardboard boxes of potatoes, cabbages, canned tomatoes and pears; dark green canisters of oxygen; an occasional truck of freshly laundered linens.

There was no laundry service at the home, so everything had to be sent out; you washed out your own underwear and were yelled at if you failed to keep your panties clean and free of discharge and bloodstains. *Let's pretend, Girls, let's pretend you aren't even here for this purpose.* You slept on your bed linens for a month and then were given a new set that smelled of scorched cloth. In her thirties, when Hazel was hospitalized for pneumonia, she had to beg the nurses to cover the hospital sheets with a blanket, the torturous scent dragging her back to that time.

She had never married. Her parents welcomed her when their driver dropped her back at home. She could still feel that day, like a crack in her ribs, a wound that punctured her lungs altering how she breathed. The grandfather clock thrumming the hour as she opened the thick front door. The screen door escaping from her fingers into the wind so that it slammed and vibrated—an angry slap throughout the house.

They were at the dining room table. A bouquet of blood-red roses crowned the sideboard, spreading a too sweet odor over her father's lingering pipe smoke. Thick water glasses clunked with ice and slices of lemon as they raised their glasses when they saw her in the arched frame of the doorway.

"Hazel, welcome."

They were a Greek chorus. Her father ducked his head back into the Detroit Free Press. Her mother rose from her chair:

"What a lovely salmon color on you. I declare I don't know where they find such clothing. We're having omelets."

She was only sixteen. The baby had been born at the height of summer, on a day when Hazel's body was fecund and round and she had walked the periphery of the woods alone. The gardener at the place had always watched out for her, talked to her, singling her out from the other girls who seemed to find a friend in one another. Hazel never did. On that birth day the gardener, a tall man with a moustache and dirty fingernails, had handed her a bouquet of Queen Anne's lace, plucked from the hot soils at the edge of the vegetable garden, far away from the building. She had thanked him and wandered off, imaging that when her child was born, the gardener would come and stand at the door of the so-called sterile room and smile at her; he would offer to love her and her child. In time he would drive the two of them away from the place, away to a cottage where red roses and Queen Anne's lace twined along a fence. Their child would run barefoot through the warm soil of a kitchen garden, extend a starfish hand crushing mint leaves, and tossing smiles and laughter toward them both.

Such thoughts she had played with as the first pain crept from her back and sprung around, clamping down on her belly. The first of many.

When Did My Mother Die?

Ruth was awake, not wanting to be, but awake. Dan was softly snoring next to her, their upper arms touching, so that his sonorous noises almost vibrated through her. But her thoughts went immediately to her mother—the ninety-six-year-old probably having her breakfast, sitting in her wheelchair, her hair flat against the bones of her head, her hand trembling, raising the lukewarm cup of coffee.

No aid had called during the night—no Kathy, Betty, Mary. (Ruth was glad her mother had not named her any of those "y" names, the names of her peers.) She got out of bed and stretched. She had slept well and Dan had—still was. This, the pattern of her nights and days, the ups and downs: how was mom or how mom was. When to plan—anything; or how to plan anything.

But you're so fortunate to still have her.

Ruth padded down the stairs, the words of a friend beating in her head like an insistent mantra. She was a bad daughter. She would call the senior home later today and try to talk to her mother. But in the last few months that had become more and more difficult. Sometimes Ruth hung on the phone listening to her mother's breathing, saying "Mom, it's Ruth. Mom, I love you. Mom how are you. Mom, it's Ruth." More breathing. And in the background lots of talking and laughter and sometimes wailing, because Mom was in the bullpen—the large area by the nurses' station where the aids gathered all the residents in their wheelchairs and kept them busy before dinner. Sometimes Ruth could hear Frank Sinatra singing in the background or Lucy Ricardo squawking at Ethel. If the residents were calm on a given evening, there were threads of a song from the upright piano in the dining room. Then Ruth knew the supercilious music director of the home had stopped by to "entertain"—his attitude one of distain. But he was there.

It seemed only weeks ago that Mom could really talk on the phone, though she no longer answered the call with her warm familiar phrase, "Oh, is this my Ruth?" She spoke often of traveling—she had just gotten off a bus. She was on a cruise. She was packing her suitcase.

Now she would kind of growl into the phone, soft guttural sounds—or there would be just the breathing...

In the kitchen it was eight a.m. On the fridge granddaughter Katie always smiling, missing her two front teeth in her Kindergarten photo. Beautiful, bright and so loving—Ruth's DNA. Mom's too.

Ruth started the coffee, spread the morning paper on the counter.

What's it like to be inside Mom's brain, to not really hear, despite her five thousand dollar hearing aids, what is going on around her; to not remember what day it is. To bump along missing things—kernels gone on the corncob, freight cars missing from the freight train. Ruth's and Mom's relationship a living-necklace, slowly losing, dropping a bead. One by one.

It was just five years ago that Ruth would stay with

Mom in her condo. And because there was only one bedroom, Ruth slept in the other twin bed, opposite Mom—an experience Mom seemed to love, probably bringing back memories of child Ruth asking to climb in and snuggle because of a bad dream or a belly ache. Mom was everything then, protection and love.

Adult Ruth, her breasts round and soft in her granny gown, missed Dan, faked sleep when Mom, with creaky, bent-over movements, got up in the night to urinate, her body blurting out gas as she moved. Then Ruth wished herself somewhere else, for herself, but more for her mother's dignity.

But it was their routine, along with the five-hour drive between their two cities. Ruth drove, with her books-on-tape, to love Mom, touch her and hug her, share photos and food, take her to church and the pharmacy, make sure she was okay in the condo. After the move to the senior home, it was more of the same—until Mom's falls.

Then Ruth gripped the wheel, the car silent except for the cell phone calls that interrupted her steady view of the road. She had to hurry, get to the hospital because of the diagnosis: broken hip, cracked pelvis, and syncope from high blood pressure. Once, on the cell phone, the doctor whose first language was not English—exclaiming "Oh, oh, your mother. Your mother. She fell out bed. Just now. Ah, she might cracked something else."

Ruth had yelled, "Discharge her. Just discharge her!" She held back the swear words that she wanted to shout at the doctor. How could you let an old woman with a cracked pelvis fall out of bed—and you are RIGHT THERE.

The senior home received Mom warmly. After a day of Medicare forms and visits with the physical therapist, nurses and social worker, Ruth escaped to her car and crossed the miles back to home—back to another state.

Crossing that border often brought back the one "scene" in Mom's life—the time she stood, hands on the car's window ledge, and leaned in to Dan: "I'll never forgive you for taking my daughter away from me," Mom said. This when it was finally done and he had accepted the new position, the new opportunity, the next step up the ladder. This after fifty years of weekly devotion—but yes, Ruth was leaving Mom.

There would be discussions about Mom joining them. And they all ended in: "I've got Teresa to call if I need help." But that wasn't it.

Mom's people were all buried just miles from her condo. The street signs and stoplights, the clanging of the railroad crossing bells, the placement of stores and shops, of hairdresser and doctor offices, the path to her church—these were part of the grooves in Mom's brain and you just could not remove her from the familiar, the secure, the memory. And then one day, after a heated discussion, it was sealed: "I will *never* leave Chicago." Okay.

As the pelvic bone healed, Mom began to know again where she was, though her pain didn't have a memory. Monday: referred sciatic pain down her left leg and Mom yelling, "Cut it off, my leg, cut it off." But two weeks later, when asked about her pain, "What pain. There's nothing wrong with me."

And "new" had no memory either. "New" just didn't work for Mom: the new walker, wheel chair alarm, bed alarm and physical therapy routines. For Ruth it all meant tears on arrival and tears on departure—waiting, praying for the elevator door to open so the tears could begin. Then the five-hour drive back home. *You're so fortunate to still have her.*

Once, when Ruth was due to leave early in the morning, her suitcase packed and her cell phone charged, she had a bad dream. It woke her instantly. But all she could remember was an angry voice—was it a male voice—trying to hold back some fury. The out-of-control tones blocked the rest of the dream, so Ruth just got up. Downstairs, the newspaper already bloomed on the front porch. She made coffee, thinking no human could hold within himself or herself such an angry cadence. But she hurried to dress and leave, pushing the dream aside, the day sucking her in, her hands gripping the steering wheel—or she might never have gone at all. That's how it was.

But today was a good day, a sunny blue-sky day, with a few fluffy white clouds making Ruth smile as she ran errands and then taught a class on diet and exercise at the health department. This work was the last vestige of her nursing career. This she could still do despite journal articles about dementia or drugs for Alzheimer's piled on her bedside table. It was too late for this information to help Mom or her Aunt Cecile who died five years ago. But dementia runs in families, so when Ruth would forget where she put her glasses, she might break out in a sweat of worry. Or was it a hot flash.

Ruth had tried to educate Mom the year before Cecile died:

Dear Mom,

I know you are troubled by Cecile's dementia and I wish I could say something to make it better. Every day when you visit will be the same. She's not going to get better, only worse. But deep inside, despite her confusion and desire to constantly sleep is the same loving sister you've known your whole life. She's the same heart who read to you as a child, braided your hair, paid for my piano lessons and brought cakes to all our birthday parties. And we don't know how long she'll be with us, so just enjoy her. You can't make her better, so hold her hand and reminisce about old times. Some days she'll be right there with you. Talk about your mother and father, your home on Elm. See what she remembers as her long-term memory is still there—you just have to awaken it. She won't remember what she ate at lunch and when she points to her hearing aids—don't get frustrated. She cannot explain things that are complicated. She is child-like now and you love her despite that.

Try pretending Cecile is me and I've been in a terrible car crash and can't remember anything. You wouldn't go into my room and be angry with me. You would understand and sit and hold my hand or bring me a flower or a picture or a piece of cake. You would try to make me happy while you were with me. So do that for Cecile. The calm you bring her will calm you. Yelling at her won't help at all, only hurt her and hurt you.

See you soon, Ruth

This was during the time Mom would get on the phone and brag about how she yelled at Cecile for forgetting something. It made Ruth want to pull away.

"I have a dirty little secret," she told Dan. "Whenever I can, while ironing or doing brainless stuff, I watch reruns of JUDGING AMY. I want the mother in that show, Maxine Grey, to be my mother. Oh the character is moody and ornery, but she gets it, she uses her mother-bear instincts in all the right ways. Once, I watched it with Mom. In the episode this bizarre character, Donna, is going through labor in a tub in Amy's living room. Donna's mother arrives, angry because she found out about the pregnancy at the very last moment. When she decides to leave, to miss the birth, Maxine lets her have it: 'You don't get to give up,' she shouts. 'That's your child in there in pain, experiencing the most important day of her life. You can't give up on her.' But the woman does and so Maxine, anger flaring from every pore in her body, goes to Donna, kneels down beside her and helps birth the baby. Tears filled my eyes. Mom wanted to turn it off. Left the room. She's so damn wedded to her generation, being knocked out for my birth. Sometimes I'm afraid of her and her ideas and I don't think she really truly knows who I am!"

Dan was silent for a long time. Then he reached over and folded Ruth's hands in his. "She loves you. And she knows and understands the things about you that she needs to know to feed her love for you. Forget the rest of it. She's old. It's not fair of you to want her to keep up, to change. You won't either."

Ruth had opened her mouth to object, but then just sighed and leaned over, kissed him. "She's a survivor, so stubborn."

"And you too."

"No, Dan. Listen. She'll never die. I mean, she just can't relax and let go. Remember that essay she showed us, the freshman college piece? It was so pie-in-the-sky and breezy. I had to laugh. That wasn't her. She must have cheated. It was somebody else's, not my hands-clenched, *I'll never give up Mom*."

"Of course she wrote it. Her younger self did. You get that, Ruth. She's lived over seventy years since. Life works at us. Your dad died early on. She had to get tough."

Ruth let go his hands, fell against the back of the sofa. "At the senior home, she's always on her guard, ready to see through their vibe. She won't be fooled by any of it. She's my very own geriatric. My very own."

"It's okay. You can handle this."

"Yes," Ruth said trying to calm down, "yes." *I'm so fortunate to still have her.*

A week later the phone rang mid-morning. Ruth got the voice fairly quickly, its soft tones now raspy with medication, pain and aging. Eleanor was Mom's closest and dearest Chicago friend. Older and more flexible than Mom, the ninety-seven-year-old woman read widely, loved politics and was always vocal about helping people and accepting change. Eleanor knew how to listen and Ruth loved her—in fact when she thought about it, Eleanor was more *Maxine Grey* than Mom. But the woman's life had been easier in many ways, allowed her more time to let the world in and consider her options, adapt to newer thinking.

"How are you, Ruth?"

"The better question, how are you."

"Well longevity is not for the weak. But you already know that. You're a nurse."

Oh those words. How many times had Ruth heard them? In the hospital at midnight, Christmas Eve for God's sake, when Mom had a TIA, the first real clue that her brain was suffering from ischemic attacks. Dan and Ruth, already in Chicago, raced to be with her.

"You're a nurse! Why did you let this happen?"

were Mom's first words; a reflection of the TIA? Or was this what the woman expected—that Ruth could keep her whole. For Mom was having nothing of debilitating change. Rather than read about health and adjust her diet or take a walk, she railed against Cecile's hearing loss, talked often about her friend, Tom, a World War II vet whose cancer surgery left a crater in his neck. Mom might have lost Dad early on, but she was going to cheat death and everything else that went with it.

Now maybe even dear Eleanor was assuming too much. Ruth knew only that the woman was bed-ridden in her home, cared for by three rotating aids, and visited by her large and loving family who showed up, whenever, at her bedside.

"Can you still read, Eleanor?"

"No. But I watch movies, the news. All day. And I nap. I eat very little. How's Mom?"

"Lost. She's just lost."

"She misses that sister."

"More to the point, she misses hanging out with you, but now it's so bad she really doesn't know what or who she misses."

"Oh Ruth, we were like sisters. We were. And you know, I wasn't always easy on her, though she can be sensitive but stubborn. At the same time. But I had to tell her a few years back—that she had terrible breath. We figured out she wasn't cleaning her partial denture well. And you, you're her daughter. You should have been the one to tell her. It should have been you."

Ruth turned to stare out at the bare trees bathed in wispy winter sunlight. Cinnamon. During that time she had bought Mom some cinnamon-flavored mints, but never gave them to her. Never said a word.

"You're right, but—"

"Ruth, your mother shouldn't come to see me anymore. Tell Teresa or whoever you have hired to be you—not to bring her. She can't carry a conversation. She just sits and stares at me. I don't want to see her anymore."

Heat, a hot flash, surging. "But you're her best friend. Eleanor, please. She relied on you for guidance, stuff I just couldn't do. Like the denture thing. Like how to dress when you're ninety, or that time you went to the condo and advised her about new drapes and…"

"No. It's better this way Ruth. My decision. Better."

There were birds now, alighting in the trees, all landing at once, heavy dark fruit on the branches. Ruth said quietly, "I'll try to see you next time."

"Oh it's getting late for me. Late. I don't know. But. So. So which is better, Dear Ruth. You're a nurse. Knowing what's happening or being in that big fog?"

For a moment maybe Maxine Grey was back, the voice, tender again, losing its edge. Tears formed in Ruth's eyes. She didn't want this Eleanor to leave her.

"I don't know. I don't have any answers. It's all very, I mean I know it's just very hard. I want to say things to you. Before. Like thank you for being Mom's friend, being my friend. Thank you for all the great talks we had and there was so much laughter. And you always liked me. I love you Eleanor."

"I love you too. I love your mother. She was the best friend to me, bright and warm, fun to be with. Smart. Not like any other friend I ever had. And she loves you so much."

The birds were scattering now, climbing up the watery sky.

"So bye now, Ruth. Be good, take care of her for me," and the call ended.

Ruth turned away, sobbing.

But you're so fortunate to still have her.

ABOUT ELIZABETH A. HAVEY

A mother of three adult children, Elizabeth A. Havey now has the time to publish the stories and novels she has written and revised over the years. Graduating with a BA in English, Havey taught literature at the secondary level and later worked part time as a freelancer for McDougal Littell Publishing and proofreader for Meredith Books. In her early forties, she earned her RN and worked as a labor and delivery nurse, health educator and author of CEUs for nursing. Summers found her studying at the Iowa Summer Writing Workshops at the University of Iowa. Her short stories have appeared in little magazines including *The Nebraska Review* and *Zinkzine*. Havey welcomes you to read and follow Boomer Highway at http://boomerhighway.org, a blog devoted to health and navigating the third act. You can also find her on www.elizabethahavey.com, her author site devoted to fiction. Born, raised and educated in Chicago, Havey now lives in Southern California, but the spirit of the Midwest remains fresh in her fiction. She is a member of the Women's Fiction Writers Association.

Find more good books at

Foreverland Press
www.foreverlandpress.com

21113117R10086

Made in the USA
San Bernardino, CA
07 May 2015